JOURNEY PROUD

SALLEY MCADEN MCINERNEY

For Michael, Skipper, Mac, Ella Pearl and the children of the Triangle. Without each of you riding shotgun in some sure and steady way, this journey would have been impossible.

And for Lee, whose determined back-seat driving made me believe in where I was bound.

Thanks to Jill McCorkle and Beverly Gibbons, my first readers; Dr. Edmund Taylor, Dr. Jerald Winakur and Dr. Julian Adams, who advised me on medical issues and the state of medicine for minorities in the 1960s in Columbia; Dr. Warner M. Montgomery, who advised me on the state of public education in the 1960s in Columbia; Brian P. Fahey, who advised me on the integration of parochial schools in South Carolina; Kathleen Parker, Tom McLean and Bobby Hitt, who encouraged me to write; Dennis Cobb, for his technical support and patience; and Tina Mayland, whose artwork graces the cover of this book.

PART ONE

CHAPTER ONE

Annie Hart woke up every morning at 6:00 a.m. This morning was no different. She opened the blinds in her bedroom, peed in the bathroom with his and her sinks scalloped like cockleshells, and went to the kitchen to plug in the pot-bellied coffee percolator. There was a dent in its stainless steel body and a deep chip on its glass knob. This was the percolator Annie threw across the kitchen when she and Tom fought about who would get it when they parted ways. It was a stupid fight, but it was a good coffeepot. Made strong, hot joe.

Annie slid her fingertip down the broken edge of the knob. There had not been a morning since her divorce two years ago that she hadn't done this. She wondered if she wanted to cut herself, an odd thing troubled teens were doing these days. Annie read somewhere that cutting released something painful inside the cutter and that created a pleasurable feeling.

She pressed her fingertip harder against the glass edge, but it did not break the skin.

While the percolator grumbled, Annie went outside to retrieve the newspaper from wherever the deliveryman had tossed it in the front yard. Grown men and women driving beat-up cars delivered the *Record* these days, not boys on bikes with canvas sacks slung across their shoulders.

The *Record* had landed in the pansy bed, smashing two of the velvety flowers. It was the

Wednesday edition, pregnant with inky advertising inserts. Annie was pregnant only once, three years into the marriage.

She'd hardly bled. Only a cramp or two prefaced the miscarriage. A clump of fetal tissue floated to the bottom of the toilet bowl in the guest bathroom. Annie reached for it in the pink water. It was slippery, like a minnow. Gray and sinewy. She wanted to smell it, but resisted, letting it slide from her hand back into the water. She felt a rush of sadness, but then, relief. Not wanting—not *deserving*—a baby was a truth about herself that only Annie understood. How could she possibly explain that to anyone?

On the day he asked for a divorce, Tom suggested they take a walk down to the dock. The air was crisp; the sky cerulean. Annie grabbed the plaid throw off the den sofa and followed her husband down the path to the lake. She and Tom had moved out of Columbia to nearby Lake Murray many years ago. Once there,

Annie'd started her life over as a loner, freed from committee meetings, social engagements, and friends who were having babies.

On the dock, Tom pulled two folding chairs from the storage box where they kept their lake gear. Skis. Ropes. Life vests. Half-used bottles of SPF 30. A moldy towel or two. The water on the lake was silky. A kingfisher chattered in the distance.

"What a beautiful afternoon," Annie said.

"I'm leaving," Tom replied.

"Leaving?" Annie asked, even though she knew what he meant.

"I want a divorce."

"Why?"

"You know why."

"No children?"

"Not just that. No wife either."

Tom didn't speak spitefully, just matter-of-factly.

"Is there someone else?"

"Annie, please, this is about you and..."

"Never mind."

So what if there is someone else? Annie thought. She pulled the throw tighter around her shoulders. She wasn't surprised by his request. She was simply empty; played out. It was true what Tom said. They hadn't had sex in years; Annie didn't even like Tom touching her. They had become roommates. Sharing the same space, trying not to annoy each other.

"I'm sorry, Tom."

"Me too."

"So how do we do this?"

Tom, an attorney, said it would be easy as long as they could agree on the big things—the money, the house, and the boat. Annie waited for him to finish, stood up, folded her chair, and put it in the storage box. Tom reached out to touch her hand, but she pulled away. Always, she pulled away. At the house, she took an Ambien and went to bed. She didn't know what time Tom came up from the dock, but when he did, he slept in the guest bedroom, as usual, under the ruse that he didn't want his snoring to keep her awake.

Annie pinched the blossoms off the crushed pansies and reached for the newspaper. She could call and complain, but even if she was lucky enough to get a real person on the phone, who would listen to a middle-aged woman bitching about her flowers? No one.

Back inside the house that had become hers in the divorce settlement, Annie poured a cup of coffee and returned to her bedroom. The routine suited her. Much better, really, than having to share the paper with another person. Especially now that the newspaper had gotten so small.

The largest headline offered more news about Henry Porter's historic run for the governorship of South Carolina. Porter, a Democrat, was a black man, and if that wasn't intriguing enough, questions were surfacing about his parentage. The Republican camp was pressing Porter about it, smug with its own Ken-doll candidate. The media was circling like buzzards above carrion. But Porter was holding firm. He offered no details about the man who fathered him. He insisted on privacy for his mother, whom he called a "single mom who worked hard to raise me" and who had yet to appear in the newspaper or on TV.

Annie liked Porter—especially his dedication to the environment. She'd vote for him. In the meantime, she hoped his handlers knew how important the subject of family was around these parts. Who you were and where you came from was no small matter in South Carolina.

Annie took a sip of coffee, perusing the other headlines. A small one in the lower right-hand corner of the front page startled her: OLD MONTAGUE FARM TO BE DEVELOPED.

The article was brief.

The Congaree Development Group announced Tuesday that it has purchased a 300-acre farm located in Richland County, just outside the city limits of Columbia. Yesterday's transaction, estimated by several sources at $30 million, paves the way for commercial development of a tract of land that has long been left in its natural state.

The valuable property had been held for many years by descendants of Manning Montague, a successful horse breeder and avid naturalist. During his lifetime, Montague steadfastly refused to sell the land.

**At a news conference held yesterday at
Congaree Development's headquarters
on Main Street, company president John
Thompson said development of the property
would begin "immediately, with clearing of
acreage on a spectacular bluff, where construction of luxury two- and three-bedroom
condominiums is planned."**

**Chiles Montague, a Columbia businessman,
said his family was pleased with the company's plans for the property. "As it is, there's
nothing out there other than a falling-down
barn, some old cornfields and plenty of
kudzu. It will be good to see the property
revitalized."**

"Revitalized, my ass," Annie hissed.

She tossed the newspaper on the floor, leaned
her head against the bedstead, and closed her
eyes.

A falling-down barn? Old cornfields? Kudzu?
There was so much more out there than that.

11

What about First Field? Full of deer paths that wound like a maze through the waist-high broom grass. Or the high bluff that fell off into wide, wild bottomlands where thunderstorms rumbled through like army tanks and bobcats screamed like banshees? Or what about the massive sky that came alive every fall with the flight of black grackles? Hundreds of them, blurring the heavens with their blackness, flying south for the winter. But best of all, the Old Lady, a massive Southern live oak tree whose barrel-like branches dipped to earth and then reached again for the sky.

The Old Lady was much more than a tree. She was a mother, her arms inviting Annie and her neighborhood friends in among her branches. Annie was thirteen the last time she saw the tree. Her big brother, Will, had died in a car accident, and Annie couldn't believe things could get any worse, but they did.

It wasn't just that Annie's mother locked herself in Will's room, curled up like a stove coil in her brother's bed, forgetting that she still had another child, a child who needed her. And it wasn't that Annie's father sent her mother off to "get some rest" at a "nice place" in Maryland, which Annie knew was nothing more than a few fancy steps up from the State Hospital on Bull Street.

And it wasn't even that Naomi Portee, the color of caramel, came to take care of Annie in her mother's absence. No, it was what happened when Annie believed nothing else could happen.

They huddled inside the old barn at the Montague farm on a chilly March afternoon in 1964. Annie, Buck, Briddy, and Twig. A rare, stupendous snowfall had closed school. The farm had turned into a sea of glistening, rolling white. They had spent the day sledding down the bluff and building a snowman when, in the late afternoon, Briddy cried out, grasping her belly.

Inside the dark, cavernous barn, Briddy clenched her teeth. Sweat rolled down her face, disappearing into her rampant red hair. The heavy horse blanket that covered her smelled of animals. Briddy was barely sixteen.

Twig was twelve. His eyes were shut so hard his face looked like a shriveled peach. He knelt beside Briddy, his knees pressing into the fecund earth of the barn floor. He wore a pair of his father's work gloves. They were blue and way too big for his small hands, which were clasped in front of his chest. He was praying.

Then there was Buck. He had a perfectly round brown mole just below his left earlobe. He was a year older than Annie, and he was the one who took charge. He stationed himself between Briddy's legs. Annie saw a mound of pubic hair. Orange, like a wooly little pumpkin. Annie could not imagine a man being where Buck was now. He pressed Briddy's knees apart and cupped his hands as a tiny creature slid out of Briddy's insides. It happened so quickly. Annie

14

could hardly breathe, as if the atmosphere had suddenly emptied of air. Buck cut the blue, ropey cord with his Boy Scout knife.

Not long before, the school nurse had gathered the sixth graders in the school cafeteria—first the girls, then the boys—to discuss the subject of reproduction. If the scratchy film *You and Your Body* was supposed to be anything like what was happening here, then something had gone wrong. Way wrong. This flesh-and-blood business had nothing to do with those diagrams, arrows, and small red spots.

"I swear to God, Briddy, none of us will ever tell," Buck said. A slash of red from the birthing blood marked one side of his face. He held the silent infant in his arms. He had wrapped it in his favorite Yankees sweatshirt.

Annie thought she was going to be sick.

"Dern it, y'all, we won't tell, will we?" Buck implored, his voice rising.

"No," Annie cried, "we won't."

Briddy shivered. Her eyes were closed, her head turned away from them all. Annie picked a piece of straw from her hair.

"But what about the baby?" Twig whispered.

His hands were still clasped together. Twig wanted to be a Catholic saint when he grew up. Last summer he had ridden his bike to the public library every Saturday morning and spent several hours there investigating which saint he could be. Annie had gone with him, reading the Black Stallion books while Twig, aided by a bemused librarian, did his research. Twig determined that the patron saint of clean sheets had not been claimed. He was not kidding about this. His eyes were big and brown and serious when he explained to Annie that if there were saints to help human beings solve other problems—and he knew every problem and every appropriate saint—then why not one who aided in the plight of pissing in your sheets?

Annie knew Twig spoke from experience; he wet his bed almost every night. Occasionally, he wet his pants in broad daylight.

"Buck," Twig whispered again, "what about the..."

"There ain't no baby," Buck growled. "You got that? Everybody got that? There can't be no baby, so there *ain't* no baby."

"But," Twig blurted, "there *is* a baby." He made the sign of the cross and began a prayer to Saint Jude, the patron saint of hopeless situations.

Buck pushed the baby into Annie's arms. He grabbed Twig's jacket, twisting it into a tight wad around the small boy's throat. "You quit that praying shit and you listen to me. I said there ain't no baby. Now you say that back to me."

Twig didn't say anything; Buck wrenched the jacket tighter.

Annie held the baby close to her chest. It felt supple, like a water balloon. "Please, Buck," she whispered, "let Twig go."

"I gotta hear him say it first," Buck demanded.

"There ain't no baby," Twig mumbled.

"No, I wanna hear it loud and clear."

"There ain't no baby!" Twig screamed at the barn rafters, jerking himself away from Buck.

"Good. Now you and Annie go on home. I'll take care of Briddy. She'll be OK."

Briddy moaned.

"Are you sure we should go?" Annie asked Buck. "I mean, we can stay and..."

"I'm sure," Buck replied, reaching for the shovel he'd made Twig retrieve from a stall in the barn. The shovel had a worn handle and a rusty face.

"Buck?" Annie whispered.

"Give me the baby and just git, OK? Please, just git."

Annie fought the urge to run from the barn with the baby safely clutched to her chest. She'd always been able to outrun Buck.

"Annie?" Buck was glaring at her.

She swallowed hard and put the infant into Buck's hands, noticing for the first time the baby's crown of hair. Curly, like Briddy's, but black, like somebody else's.

"Com'on, Twig," Annie said, standing up. The boy rose from the barn floor. He took a deep breath and squared himself to Buck, setting his feet wide apart.

"Th-th-this isn't right," he stammered.

Buck's eyes—blue, like the color of the Tiffany box Annie kept her arrowhead collection in—did not blink.

"Nothing about this is right," Buck replied. "Now, leave."

Annie and Twig obeyed.

"I'm gonna tell the Old Lady good-bye," Twig said, standing outside the barn, looking toward the bluff.

"Good-bye?" Annie asked.

"I'm never coming back here."

Twig crunched across the hardening snow toward the bluff. His father's work boots poked potholes in the snow. The Old Lady stood sentry over the late-afternoon landscape. The sky was lavender. The Old Lady looked like she had been dressed in cotton. Twig reached as far around her trunk as he could.

"I gotta go now," he murmured, pressing his body against the tree, "but I wanted to say thanks for everything. I love you."

Twig kissed the Old Lady, turned, and began walking across First Field toward home.

"You coming?" he called over his shoulder to Annie.

Annie ran after her friend, and when they reached the barbed wire fence that separated the farm from Annie's backyard, Twig stepped on it so Annie could walk over it. She did the same for him.

"I reckon that's it," Annie said when they were both on the other side of the fence.

"You reckon that's it?" Twig cried.

"Well." Annie's voice was limp.

"Well *what*? Briddy just had a baby and Buck's out there letting it die and getting ready to bury it and all you got to say is 'That's it?' "

"How do you know it's even alive? It didn't wiggle when I was holding it and it didn't make

21

any noise. Aren't babies supposed to holler when they're born?"

"Maybe it didn't make any noise, but it was alive. I know it was alive and I know what's about to happen out there is... Well, shit, Annie..."

"We can't help it," Annie mumbled. "I gotta go."

"We can too help it. We can go back there."

"I said I gotta go."

Annie opened her eyes and reached for her coffee. It was cold. She set the mug back on the bedside table and pulled herself deep down into her covers. She wrapped her arms around her knees, tucked her head into the warm, round space her shape made. She could feel her breath. It was warm, wary.

She waited for the specter of that last day on the farm to pass from her chest, where it banged around like a crazed inmate, and back down into her gut, where it lived like a hermit. Then she sat up, retrieving the newspaper from the floor.

Annie pulled the front page from the rest of the paper and folded it carefully into quarters. She would save it. That amounted to putting it on a pile on her desk in the den. Bills, how-to articles, two-for-one coupons, a wedding invitation that necessitated a reply and a present, and a rare, handwritten thank-you note for a contribution of her artwork to a charity fundraiser. Save for the bills, the pile would continue to grow until the day it suddenly got on her nerves.

Annie checked the bedside clock. Not even 7:00 a.m. She unfolded the front page and read the article again.

It had all begun in late August 1963. The Columbia heat was so bad TV weatherman Beau Finner fried an egg on the sidewalk in front of the State House downtown. Businessmen stirred their morning coffee at the Friendly Cafeteria on Main Street and said the weather was bound to break by September.

On the outskirts of the city, in the neighborhood of Shimmering Pines, the heat was just as bad, but there were convivial respites, when the weather was forgotten and the world was joyful. Word circulated fast when a family got a new car, color television set, or central air-conditioning. Everybody was offered a ride around the block in the new car; everybody was invited to come see the new TV or feel the amazing cool.

Dogs found shelter from the sun behind azalea bushes, digging deep holes in the dirt. On Saturday mornings, mothers did their "big shopping" at Colonial Grocery and fathers put on shorts, discovered the holes, cussed at the dogs, and mowed withered grass. On Sundays, families went to church.

On Monday mornings, fathers returned to work, relieved to get back to offices with secretaries who smiled pleasantly and smelled of L'Air du Temps perfume. No matter what day of the week, mothers wished for the school year to begin.

Children just got bored, poking their heads inside Kelvinator refrigerators to see if there was something to eat that hadn't been there five minutes before. They got fat, red chigger bites along their underpants lines and they stubbed their toes riding their bikes barefooted.

Maids came and went to Shimmering Pines on dirty city buses. They pulled a cord above their heads to request their stops and then they stepped off into another world. They walked down the street together, sharing last bits of gossip before leaving each other at the ranch-style homes where they were employed. They were called by their first names—Flossie, Ivy, Viola. They cooked, cleaned, and kept track of children. They ironed shirts, using Niagara spray starch, and they hung laundry out on backyard lines. If a thunderstorm threatened in the early afternoon, they hitched up their uniforms around their hips and raced to get the drying clothes before the rain came. In the late afternoon, they left the same way they had come—on city buses bound for the other side of town.

For all this, the maids made $35 a week. Slightly more if they worked a half day on Saturdays. Most maids in Shimmering Pines wore white uniforms. Only one wore blue. Her name was Naomi Portee.

CHAPTER TWO

Naomi Portee loathed what she called "the walk," which began at the top of Pine Tree Way when the No. 10 city bus dropped her off in Shimmering Pines at 8:00 a.m. every morning except Sunday.

The bus belched diesel fumes and ground to a stop. Naomi and the other maids gathered their bags and rose from their seats. The floor underneath their feet was sticky with gray spots of gum. They filed past the bus driver, grasped a greasy handrail, descended three steps, and began "the walk."

It took them past the Warrens' house, on the right, where a dog resembling a ball of steel wool charged from the carport to the end of the Warren driveway, snarling at the maids who kept to the left side of the road. If they were lucky, Mrs. Warren would appear at the front door and call Fluffy in.

Naomi kept her umbrella ready in case the varmint crossed the asphalt.

"Fluffy, my fat ass," Lily Monroe grumbled, walking with Naomi. "Somebody need to poison that dog."

"And *somebody* would wind up in jail," Naomi answered.

As other maids said their good-byes and disappeared into the houses where they worked, Naomi and Lily continued to the end of the street.

Lily, who worked for the Hudsons, was Naomi's best friend. They lived in Black Bottom, a collection of shotgun houses cleaving to the banks of the Congaree River six miles across town. The Bottom was nothing like Shimmering Pines, but at least the place had personality. Naomi preferred the clapboard houses—mostly gray, some peeling vestiges of old paint—to the faceless brick homes here. She found joy in Lily's fake flowers stuck in whitewashed tires, only something sad in Mrs. Hudson's leggy geraniums struggling in clay pots.

"Well, I'll see you this afternoon if I get out from under that pile of Mr. Hudson's shirts what I got to iron," Lily said. They'd reached the Hudson house.

Naomi blanched at Lily's bad grammar, but would never correct her. She loved Lily like a sister. Lily had been her rock; she'd also been the one to tell her about the Mackey job.

"Have a good day," Naomi said.

"Huh. Now how I gonna have a good day working for the Hudsons? Did I tell you Mrs. H said I can't watch my stories no more while I's ironing?"

"You told me."

"Meanness, all it is. I ain't singed a one of Mr. H's shirts in all the years I been working for that old biddy."

"Well, I don't want to be late."

"I do," Lily responded, turning down the Hudson driveway. "What Mrs. H gonna do? Fire me? Nobody else gonna work for her. Anyway, save me a seat on the bus."

Naomi walked on to the Mackey house. Mrs. Hudson was notoriously picky; Lily's niche was being able to iron her banker husband's shirts to flat, crisp perfection.

Mr. Mackey was not nearly so concerned about his shirts. In truth, Mr. Mackey had turned over management of the house to Naomi with only a few instructions.

"I'll need you to keep up with Annie, the groceries, and the cleaning," he'd said when she'd come to the house to talk about the job. "And can you cook our supper?"

"Yes, sir," Naomi replied, "I can do that."

They'd sat at the kitchen table. Naomi studied her hands, pressed into her lap. They felt sweaty. According to Lily, the last maid to work for the Mackeys had quit after finding a Ouija board in Annie's room. She'd backed out of the house and spit on the steps ten times to keep the bad mojo inside the Mackey house from following her home.

Naomi didn't care about Ouija boards; she just needed a job.

"Yeah," Naomi could hear Lily reminding her before the interview, "and Mr. Mackey need you jus' as bad, so you remember that and go in there with yo' head up."

Naomi looked at Mr. Mackey. He reminded her of Abraham Lincoln. His expression was worn and worried. He cleared his throat, pushed back his chair, and then hesitated.

"Is there anything else?" Naomi asked.

"Well, I suppose I should tell you that Mrs. Mackey does not want anyone going in Will's room. Doesn't want anything moved or changed."

"I understand."

"Well, I'm not sure I do."

Naomi shifted in her chair. It was not her business to explain anything to Mr. Mackey, so she resisted telling him that Will's belongings might be soothing to Mrs. Mackey. Smelling his things, feeling his things, seeing his things—powerful medicine for a hurting heart. She, too, knew what it was like to press her face into a man's sweatshirt, longing for his musky smell and his earthy presence.

Her husband Luke had died several years ago, changing a woman's tire by the side of the highway. It had been dusk. A passing eighteen-wheeler swiped him off his feet and slammed him into a guardrail. Luke, a plumber, never had a chance. And Naomi never had a choice. She gave up school and began cleaning the Miracle movie theater on Main Street. It was a grotesque job. Sweeping up popcorn was one thing; picking up used rubbers was quite another. So when Lily said Mrs. Mackey had not found anyone to replace the Ouija-fearing housekeeper and that it had fallen to Mr. Mackey to find someone to take care of Annie in his wife's sudden absence, Naomi had signed on.

"Ain't gonna be easy," Lily had warned, telling her the story that all the maids in Shimmering Pines already knew: Will, the Mackey's seventeen-year-old son, had slammed his Dodge

Dart into a tree on his way home from baseball practice. Katherine Mackey had managed up until a month ago—the one-year anniversary of his death—when she locked herself inside Will's room with a bottle of sleeping pills. Mr. Mackey found her unconscious, clutching one of Will's A. C. Flora High T-shirts. The next day she was on her way to a Maryland sanitarium.

"Naomi?" Mr. Mackey's voice startled her.

"Yes, sir, I'm sorry, I was just..."

"Do you have any questions?" Mr. Mackey asked, pushing his chair back from the kitchen table.

"No, sir."

The Mackey house was at the end of the street. Save for a fallowed farm that bordered its back-yard, the place wasn't any different than other homes in the neighborhood—an orange-brick affair with a low-slung carport on one end and a two-story set of bedrooms on the other.

Naomi checked the mailbox. Sometimes Mr. Mackey forgot to get the mail. She walked down the driveway, careful of the ankle-turning gravel under her feet and aware of the taut feeling in her stomach. If she let it, her mood would darken as quickly as a summer sky blindsided by an afternoon thunderstorm.

"Damn it, woman, you've got to stop this," she murmured to herself. "It's not the Mackeys' fault you're a maid and not a teacher."

"Naomi?" Mr. Mackey called.

"Yes, sir?" Naomi quickened her step. She wasn't late, but it always worried her when he was waiting in the carport.

"Annie's still asleep. I didn't wake her up."

"Yes, sir."

35

Naomi walked through the quiet house. Everything was in its place. Naomi should have been pleased, not having to pick up, but the order seemed desolate. Naomi went downstairs to the basement, where she put her bag on top of the washing machine. Mr. Mackey had not directed her to do this, but Lily had.

"White folk don' like your things lying round," Lily said. "And don' bring your dirty clothes to wash 'til you is settled in, and then just a few. And if Mr. Mackey don' tell you where to pee, see if they got a pot in the basement. That's the one you use."

Sure enough, there was a toilet in a corner across from the washing machine. It had a rusty ring around the inside of the bowl, but it worked fine, and Naomi was able to lock the basement door for privacy.

Naomi climbed the stairs back to the kitchen. She was relieved to find the slight mess of Mr. Mackey's breakfast dishes in the sink, waiting to be put in the dishwasher. Above the sink, a window looked out into a woodsy backyard. A flash of brilliant blue flew past.

Naomi smiled. *A bluebird. The bluest blue in the world.* That's what Grandee would've said. And that's why Naomi had chosen blue uniforms from the pile of formless dresses stacked on a table in the housewares department at J. C. Penney.

Before her tenacious old heart had given out several years ago, Grandee had lived in a snug cabin on a few carefully tended acres of land outside the town of McCormick, South Carolina, some forty miles from Columbia. Naomi had spent her summers there as a little girl, away from her harried mama, whose husband had run off when Naomi was ten and who was trying to make ends meet as an attendant at an all-night Laundromat. Grandee didn't like that her only grandchild had to sleep on plastic chairs lined up against a plate-glass window pasted with ads like WANT PUSSY? CALL... Naomi chuckled to herself. She'd thought someone was giving away a cat until she told Grandee about it.

"What's so funny?" A small voice interrupted Naomi's thoughts.

"Goodness," Naomi said, turning to see Annie standing by the kitchen door. "Where'd you come from?"

"My bed."

Annie was twelve. Her hair, the color of wet coffee grounds, was still tied in two thick plaits, secured with green rubber bands that had once bound the morning paper.

"I thought we talked about taking your pigtails out at night," Naomi said. "It's terrible for your hair, especially where the rubber bands are."

"It don't bother me." Annie grabbed the end of one plait and inspected it.

"Doesn't."

"Huh?"

"It *doesn't* bother me. There's no need to use improper English."

Annie rolled her eyes; Naomi ignored it.

"What would you like for breakfast?"

"PB and J."

"Your mama would not..."

Naomi felt her mistake as fast as a slap across the face; she stepped toward Annie, but the child was too quick. "*My mama is not here!*" she screamed, running for her bedroom and slamming the door.

Naomi steadied herself against the sink. The bluebird was nowhere in sight. She took a deep breath, wiped her hands dry, walked to Annie's bedroom, and stood by the door.

"Annie?"

Nothing.

"Annie, you're right, your mother is not here. But I would like for you to have a good breakfast, and I think she would too. May I come in?"

Still, nothing.

Naomi tested the doorknob; it had not been locked. She pushed the door open and looked in. Annie was wrapped in her blankets, a pillow over her head. Naomi walked to the bed and sat on the side of it as carefully as she would perch on an antique chair.

"I don't think I like you," Annie grumbled, her voice muffled by the pillow.

"Why?"

"I don't know."

"I do."

"What?"

"I think I know why you might not like me."

40

Annie pulled the pillow away from her head. Her face was red and swollen from crying; her brown bangs were matted to her forehead.

"You do?"

"I suspect you dislike me because I am not your mother, but I'm doing some of the things your mother does, and you don't like that. You want your mama to be doing those things. You want your mama, period. But the truth is, she needs time to rest. She needs time to put Will in a place where she can still love him but where she can live without him."

"Where's that?"

"Only your mama knows."

Annie wiped her nose. A clear string of snot stretched from her nostrils to the back of her hand.

"Here," Naomi said, pulling a tissue from her uniform pocket, "let me help you."

Annie sat up.

"You know, I need to tell you something," Naomi said, picking her words carefully, like she would daffodils from a briar patch.

"What?"

"I'm sorry about your brother and I'm sorry about your mama."

"Do you think Mama will get better?"

"What's better?"

"Not crazy. Not locking herself in Will's room and taking sleeping pills and wishing she was dead."

"Is that all?"

"No."

"Then what else?"

"Remembering she still has me."

"Do you think she's forgotten you?"

"Yeah."

"Why?"

"Will got killed and she wanted to die, but I was still here, and that didn't make her want to live."

Annie's words were like a paper cut. Sharp, quick, painful.

"Well, I don't think your mama has forgotten you. But it's a little like when you're riding down the road in a car and there's a big truck in front of you. It's hard to see anything in front of it, right?"

"Yeah, Daddy always passes those trucks."

"Precisely. So let's say there's a big truck in front of your mama right now and that truck isn't a real truck, but it stands for the loss of Will. Does that make sense?"

"Sort of."

"OK, well then, if that truck is in front of your mama, can she see anything around it right now? Can she see you? Can she see your daddy?"

"No."

"So what does she need to do?"

"She needs to pass the truck."

"And she's going to pass it. And when she does, she's going to see everything out ahead of her again. She's going to see you and your daddy and all those things she saw before that truck got in front of her."

"You think so?"

"I know so," Naomi said, hoping she was right and daring to put her arm around Annie.

Annie did not resist, but settled herself against Naomi's side. Naomi was reminded of

44

a baby bird, folding its fragile wings, tucking its head, and waiting for its mama to return to the nest.

Lily reached the 6:00 p.m. bus just in time. Out of breath, she clambered aboard, slipped her coins in the toll box, and looked for Naomi.

"Back here," Naomi called.

"Whew," Lily said, collapsing onto the bench seat. "What a day. Twenty shirts. That may be a record."

"Twenty shirts? How is that possible?"

"Mr. H wear two shirts a day. One in the morning and one in the afternoon. He what Mrs. H call fastiddy...I don't know, fas-something."

"Fastidious?"

"That's it! What that mean anyway?"

"Prissy."

"Well, he sure that. How was your day?"

"Fine."

"Good." Lily closed her eyes and leaned her head against the back of the seat.

Naomi stared out the window. White neighborhoods passed by, turning into shopping centers and then the office buildings of downtown Columbia. The No. 10 bus groaned up Taylor Street. Naomi looked at the Supreme Court building on the right. Two mammoth lanterns adorned either side of the bottom-heavy edifice. Naomi chuckled, remembering a nasty little boy named Simon once telling her that the boogeyman grabbed those lanterns at night and used them to light his way as he jumped across the city's building tops.

As the bus crossed Main Street, Naomi studied the State House on her left. It was a magnificent building with, she thought, only one blemish—a Confederate flag flying atop its dome along with the flags of the United States and South Carolina.

The No. 10 coasted down the hill leading away from Main Street and toward the Bottom. Fifteen minutes later, it rumbled to the last stop on the line. Manny's was a ramshackle market that advertised FREE BEER TOMORROW on a handmade sign nailed against the storefront over a weathered church pew occupied by old men who watched the No. 10 come and go.

Naomi nudged Lily; she was sound asleep.

"What?" Lily murmured.

"We're home."

CHAPTER THREE

"I don't know why you need to wander around that old place," Naomi groused. "There's no telling what you might get mixed up in. You've got plenty of room to run around here."

Room to run, yes, Annie thought. But not to roam, and that's what the old Montague farm was for—roaming.

"Please?" Annie implored. "I'm not gonna get mixed up in anything. Besides, Buck and Twig will be there. Twig's got something he needs to talk to us about. Buck's meeting me at the fence."

Naomi sat at the kitchen table shelling peas. She shifted in her chair. Her left thumb punched through the spine of each shell and launched the emerald orbs into a bowl.

"You be careful out there," Naomi muttered, not looking up from her work. "And be home for lunch."

Annie let the screen door slam behind her. It made a sharp, satisfactory sound. She took the back steps by twos, tempted to try threes. The summer earth was pliant. It felt like a moist sponge under her bare feet. Annie ran though the deep backyard toward the barbed wire fence that separated the Mackey property from the farm. The fence had long since served its purpose. Rusted wire wrapped like tourni- quets around the trunks of trees, sagged to the ground, and tangled with scuppernong vines. Rotten posts leaned over like weary soldiers.

The early sun cast lemon scores of light through the big pines. Blessedly, the morning air was still cool.

Buck Graham and his mutt, Ugly, were waiting when Annie arrived at the fence. Ugly's stumpy tail switched back and forth with the kind of adoration he only offered Annie. It was Annie who'd chosen the somber pup from a litter of far more rowdy siblings tousling with one another in a pen at the county animal shelter. Ugly was curled up at the back of the dirty cage. His head was tucked between his front paws. He looked the color and shape of a baked potato.

"But he's not doing anything," Buck had argued. It was Buck's tenth birthday and he'd finally been allowed to get a dog.

"But he will," Annie'd insisted, "just as soon as he gets out of here."

"Where you been?" Buck asked. He'd just turned thirteen and was determined to be a

doctor when he grew up. He never went anywhere without his Boy Scout knife and was
whittling on a stick. Annie watched curly
snips of wood float to the ground; they looked
like snowflakes. She sunk her hand into Ugly's
wiry coat and gave him a rub.

"Talking to Naomi."

Buck tossed the stick into the woods. "We
better get going. Twig's probably already
there."

They crossed the fence, careful not to get
snagged by the rusty barbs. Buck led the way
along a narrow deer path that wound through
a vast field they long ago had dubbed First
Field. The tall broom grass on either side of the
path billowed softly; the saffron landscape rippled like an ocean of melted butter.

"So how's Naomi anyway?" Buck asked over
his shoulder.

"She's a pain."

"How come?"

"Well, for one thing, she didn't want me coming out here. Thinks there're plenty of places to play already."

"Then she oughta come with us some time. See the farm for herself."

"You never brought Eunice out here." Eunice Deloitte worked for the Grahams. She was a long, lean woman with skin the color of a hazelnut.

"That's different. She's old. Besides, she grew up on a farm. Hates everything about 'em. Said she's seen all the cow shit she ever wants to see and if she goes anywhere other than her house, it'll be to Detroit."

"What's in Detroit?"

"Motown."

"Well, I just don't want Naomi coming out here, OK?"

Buck turned and looked at Annie.

"Something eating you?"

"The farm just ain't her business, OK?"

"Fine," Buck muttered, "but you're acting weird."

Annie wondered if Buck was right, but it did seem like Naomi was making just about everything else her business. Naomi made her sit down the other day to talk about the "change of life." Naomi said it was time Annie started preparing to become a woman. Naomi said she might start feeling moody and her breast buds might begin to feel tender.

Annie was horrified by the conversation and hated the idea of breast buds, but there was no doubt that her flat, penny-sized nipples had flushed into something wider and softer, something similar to the round, silky pads in her mother's Revlon compacts.

The very idea hardened Annie's nipples. That horrified Annie even more. She looked down at her T-shirt and two pert dots poked against the cotton material. Annie pulled the shirt away from her chest. Maybe Naomi was right.

"Hey," Buck said, kicking a stone ahead of him in the path, "have you talked to your mom yet? I miss her brownies bad."

Annie loved this about Buck; he didn't act like her mother was crazy or that she was a subject that couldn't, or shouldn't, be talked about. Other people did, especially at church, where adults smiled down at her with pursed lips and something that resembled pity. The problem was, they never *asked* about her mother. They never *talked* about her mother. Buck did.

"They won't let her talk on the phone yet," Annie said.

"Sorry."

"It's OK."

But it really wasn't.

Annie would never forget the July afternoon she came home from Buck's house. It
had rained all day and they'd been playing
Monopoly. Annie wiped her feet on the door-
mat, stepped into the house, and closed the
door quietly behind her. Ever since Will had
died, she'd been trying to do everything just
right.

The house was quiet. Usually, Annie thought,
her mother would be in the kitchen by now,
fixing supper. But there was nothing on the
stove. The black coils felt cold. Annie walked
through the house. Everything was in its
place. The silver ashtray with the swirly letters engraved in it. The glass paperweight
in the shape of a whale, with Jonah etched
inside it. And an old book about South
Carolina plantations. All on the coffee table
in the living room. Then, in the dining room,
a dried flower arrangement in a bowl in the

center of the polished table, and on either side of the flowers, fat, brass candlesticks that Annie's mother said would someday be hers.

Annie made her way upstairs. Her parents' bedroom was at the end of a hallway filled with family photos on both walls. Maybe her mother was taking a nap.

The bedroom door was open. Annie looked for the familiar, slim shape on the four-poster bed; the pretty, long hair spread out on a white-cased pillow. But the bed was empty; the wool blanket with the satin binding Annie's mother always slept with was neatly folded at the end of the bed.

Annie walked back down the hallway. The door of her brother's bedroom, on the right, was closed. That wasn't unusual these days, but still Annie grasped the door knob and tried to turn it. The door was locked. That *was* unusual. Annie tried to turn it again. No luck. Something frightening oozed through Annie.

"Mama, are you in there?"

Silence.

Annie banged on the door with a fist and listened again.

Nothing. Nothing but the sure, slick silence of something wrong.

Annie kicked the door with her bare foot. It gave a little, but not enough. She kicked harder. Pain shot upward from her big toe to her tailbone.

"*Mama!*" Annie cried, hopping on her other foot. "*Open the door!*"

But still, nothing.

Annie hobbled down the hallway to the kitchen. She reached for the black phone hanging on the wall by the kitchen table. She dialed her father's office number. SU7-1405. Her daddy always answered his phone the same way: "Mackey here." But Annie didn't wait for that.

"Mama's locked in Will's room and she won't come out!"

"Whoa, now," her father said, "slow down, Sis."

Sometimes Annie's daddy called her Sis, even though she wasn't a sister anymore.

"She won't say anything either!" Annie cried.

"Well, maybe she's not in there. Have you looked around the house? She could be in the basement. In the laundry room? Have you looked there?"

"No, sir." Annie's heart slowed; sometimes her father's methodical nature was a good thing.

"Then go look, but don't hang up. Go look and come back to the phone. I'll be right here."

Annie dropped the receiver. It banged against the wall, hanging by its curly black cord.

Annie hopped down the narrow steps to the basement. The basement was dark; the laundry room was empty. So was the workroom.

"Mama's not down there either." Annie's words spilled into the phone. She could hear her father go still. The papers on his desk stop rustling.

"Is the station wagon in the carport?"

"Daddy, I told you already! Mama's in Will's room!"

"Now, Sis, you must..."

"Don't call me Sis! I hate that name. I'm not a sister anymore."

Mr. Mackey's voice remained calm. "You're right, I'm sorry. Now, Annie, just please listen to me."

Annie blinked back tears. She grasped the phone harder. A trace of purplish blue was surfacing at the place where her big toe connected to her foot.

"Daddy, I kicked Will's door so hard I think I broke my toe. I just know Mama's in there. But why would she lock the door?"

"Goddamn it," her father hissed.

Annie hardly ever heard him say a bad word. In fact, the last time her father used the GD word was when he'd been on the phone with someone from Cauthen Funeral Home, where Will's body was before it was buried.

"We don't care what goddamn color the interior fabric of the coffin is. Do you understand that? Our son is dead. Nothing else matters."

Annie grasped the telephone receiver tightly. She thought she was going to be sick. Her knees felt like feathers. She slid down the wall to a sitting position. The blue place on her toe was spreading.

"Baby," her father said, "I'm sorry, I shouldn't have said that."

"But you only say that when something bad..."

"Stop that. Now listen, is Buck around?"

"Yes, sir, we just finished playing Monopoly. I won."

"Then go to his house and wait for me. I'll come home first, get your mama up, and then come get you, all right?"

"But why..."

"Sweetie, please do as I ask."

"Yes, sir."

Annie listened to her father hang up the phone. Then she listened to the silence on the other end of the line. It sounded so empty and awful. It sounded like the house after she and her mother and father had come home from Will's funeral. Annie tried to stand up, but her stomach protested. Something thick began its ascent inside her. Lunch. A peanut butter and jelly sandwich mixed with chocolate milk here at home. Fritos and French onion dip at Buck's. Annie took a deep breath, willing the bile back down. But her stomach heaved anyway. A syrupy stream of brown vomit spewed from her mouth, flowed across the floor, and settled in a small pool around a leg of the kitchen table. The sight reminded her of the oily sawdust the school janitor used to clean up puke at school. The stuff smelled vile. The classroom was always hot, and the kid who'd upchucked was always crying.

Annie felt a fat, hot tear roll down her cheek. Then another one. She looked at the vomit again. It glowed softly, like the satin binding on her mother's favorite blanket. Annie let the telephone receiver fall from her hand. She leaned over and stretched out on the linoleum floor. It felt cool. She closed her eyes and slipped away.

At the end of First Field, on a gentle bluff, the Old Lady rose out of the ground like the grande dame of all her surroundings. She was a Southern live oak. Her trunk was an astonishing twenty-one feet in circumference. Her branches were big around as barrels, and Spanish moss, like lace, hung from her limbs.

Twig Roebuck was tucked into his favorite spot—the crotch of a high branch that required monkey-like climbing skills to reach. Twig was twelve and he was tiny. So tiny, to his great chagrin, that he was still kept off the big rides at the state fair by greasy-faced ride operators who just looked at him and laughed.

"Hey, there," Buck called out.

Twig waved him off. He was praying. His brow rested on his bent knees. His hands were clasped together in front of his face. Annie had been the one to give Twig his nickname. His real name was Nicholas, but he carried a stick with him almost everywhere he went.

"Who ya praying to?" Buck persisted, clambering into the Old Lady.

Twig crossed himself and opened his eyes.

"Saint Anthony."

"What does he do?" Annie asked, settling on a low branch.

"Helps you find things."

"What you looking for?" Buck asked.

"Someone to help me do my sheets. Our washing machine is broke."

Buck said Twig had a hair-trigger pee button. Annie's mom said it went a lot deeper than that, and she couldn't understand why Mrs. Roebuck wouldn't do something about it, like take Twig to the doctor. Henrietta Roebuck was strung as tight as tennis racket strings. She was an ardent Catholic who colored her hair in the kitchen sink and spent most of her time at church. She got hysterical when she found Twig's soiled sheets, believing she was being punished for something by way of her son's incontinence.

"I bet Naomi would do them for you," Annie offered.

"You think?" Twig's face brightened.

"I don't know for sure, but we can ask her."

"Well, let's go then," Twig said, crossing himself again and offering a whispered thank-you to Saint Anthony.

CHAPTER FOUR

Naomi studied a spot of bird doo on the windshield of Mr. Mackey's car. It was purple in the middle and spread into an array of intricate white spikes. If it wasn't for the fact that it was bird poop, it would've made a pretty picture.

Naomi shifted in her seat. The Buick sedan floated along the road like a heavy-bottomed boat. Naomi grasped her pocketbook in her lap. She felt uncomfortable, as if she needed to say something, but what? Chitchat with a white man was not something she was used to. She wondered if Mr. Mackey knew where he was going, if he had ever been to the Bottom before. Surely, he would ask if he needed directions.

Mr. Mackey kept his eyes on the road. He had called in the late afternoon hoping Naomi could stay late. An office meeting had run longer than he'd expected. If she could wait, he would take her home.

Naomi had called Lily to let her know she wouldn't be on the afternoon bus.

"Better watch that running late b'ness," Lily warned. "Next thing you know, he be asking you to live there. Did you act like you was happy to do it?"

"I suppose I did. I just said I would, but it's fine with me."

"Girl, that ain't the point. You got to run white folk a little bit better than they think they running you."

"What?"

"What I mean is, you got to make 'em think they in charge when you is really the one in charge. It ain't nothing obvious, but, you know, quiet-like. Like he won't notice."

"You mean subtle?"

"I reckon I do. Like when Mr. Mackey call and ask you to stay late. If you say, 'Yes, sir' right off the bat, he in charge. Now, if you wanna be in charge, when he call and ask you to stay late, you take a deep breath—plenty loud enough for him to hear it—and then you don't say a word. And then he gonna get worried and say something like he really need your help, and then you kinda put a little moan and groan in your voice and you say, 'Well, let me see what I can do 'cause I got a meeting at church.' And then you tell him you gonna have to call him right back. And then you wait five minutes and you call him back and you tell him you can stay late. That's you in charge."

"I see."

"No seeing about it, girl. You gotta take charge of white folk or they take charge of you."

"Well, what I've got to do right now is more laundry," Naomi said. "I'll see you when I get home."

"Fine, but you remember what I told you. I been fooling 'round white folk a lot longer than you. I know what I'm talking 'bout."

Naomi was in the laundry room when Annie and Buck burst through the back door. Annie was out of breath and announced that Briddy'd run her daddy's car into a ditch and they needed Naomi's help getting it out.

"Please," Annie pleaded. "We ain't strong enough to get it out."

"*Aren't.*"

"Aren't. But could you please, *please* help us? If Mrs. Roebuck finds out, she's gonna kill Briddy. Briddy ain't—isn't—s'posed to be driving anywhere. She's got her learner's permit, but has to drive with her mama or daddy. We went to Twig's house to get his sheets and Briddy was backing out the driveway to go to Bell's. We went with her, and when we were coming home, she was turning into her driveway and she cut too close and went into the ditch. The back end of the car's stuck, and we need to get it out before Mrs. Roebuck gets home."

Buck was standing just behind Annie. He was a stunning boy. Sun-bleached blond hair. Like the color of a clean, white mop. A dark summer tan. A smattering of freckles on his face. Aquamarine eyes.

"What do you have to say?" Naomi asked him.

"Me?"

"Yes, you."

"There's no telling what Mrs. Roebuck'll do if she finds out Briddy drove to Bell's."

"What about Mr. Roebuck? It's his car, right? Where's he?"

"Drunk asleep in his bed," Annie said. "Twig already checked. He won't wake up."

"You told me you were going to the farm," Naomi said, snapping out one of Mr. Mackey's T-shirts with a sharp crack. "Not Bell's. And not with somebody you know you shouldn't be riding with."

"We did go to the farm," Buck offered, "but then we went to Twig's to get his sheets and that's when Briddy was leaving."

"What were you doing with Twig's sheets?"

Buck looked at Annie.

"Twig wets his sheets," Annie explained. "We were gonna bring them down here and see if you would wash 'em. The Roebucks' washing machine is broke."

"Broken."

"Could you just please come help us?" Buck pleaded. "We really need your help."

Naomi followed Annie and Buck up the street. The afternoon was sultry, and the neighborhood was quiet. Front porches—constrained, concrete spaces outlined by ivy-leaved iron railing—were empty. In the Bottom, front porches were much more useful affairs, offering enough room for a swing, several mismatched chairs, maybe an old appliance, and easy conversation in the aftermath of another workday.

The Roebuck house was not far; it looked much like the Mackey house, save for a turquoise front door with a star-shaped doorknob and a concrete birdbath that had fallen over near the front shrubs.

Sure enough, the right back end of Mr. Roebuck's Plymouth station wagon was settled comfortably down in the ditch, like an old man asleep in an easy chair. A plank had been placed over a large rock and then wedged underneath the tire. Twig was perched on the high end of the plank. His banty weight was not nearly enough to make the lever system work.

Briddy sat on the grassy embankment. She was beautiful, with long, flaming-red hair. She was fifteen and going on fearless. Naomi could not take her eyes off the girl. It was the hair, she decided. God-given, gorgeous, and a portent of perilous things to come.

"Thanks for coming," Briddy said, untangling her slender legs and standing up. "I'm Briddy."

Naomi met the girl's eyes. "You're welcome."

"Think we can get it out?" Twig asked, still perched on the board.

Naomi walked around the car once, her arms crossed.

"I think we can," Naomi said. "Whose idea was the rock and the plank?"

"Mine," Twig said, a toothy smile usurping his solemn face. "We studied lever systems in school last year."

Naomi assessed her manpower. One person was needed to steer the car, the rest to push on the plank. Naomi looked at Twig. The scrawny child had no meat on his bones; his wrists and knees stuck out like galls on a tree limb. But he had an adult-like sense about him, some kind of premature determination born of being so small.

"Can you reach the pedals of the car?" she asked him.

Twig jumped down from the plank and puffed up like an adder. "Damn right, I can."

"There's no need to use foul language."

"Sorry," Twig said, crossing himself.

Naomi ignored the odd gesture. "Follow me."

Naomi went around to the front of the car, sat in the driver's seat, and turned the key in the ignition. The white station wagon grumbled to a start. She pulled the seat forward as far as it would go.

"All right, then, when I say go, I want you to press down on the accelerator. But not before I say go, and not too hard. We don't want the tires spinning, we want them to catch. The rest of us are going to lean on the plank and push the end of the car up enough to get it rolling. Got it?"

"Yes, ma'am."

"As soon as we get it out of the ditch, stop. We'll let your sister take it up the driveway."

"Yes, ma'am, but..."

"But what?"

"Do I have time for a prayer?"

"A prayer?"

"To Saint Expedite. He helps rush prayers to God. And I'm praying we get this car out of the ditch before Mama gets home."

"Well, I suppose," Naomi said, not sure what else to say.

Twig bowed his head and mumbled a prayer to the saint of rushing things through. He climbed into the car and shimmied his bottom as close to the edge of the seat as possible.

"Are you sure you can reach?" Naomi asked.

"Sure as shi...shooting."

Naomi returned to the back of the station wagon and grasped the end of the plank. Briddy, Buck, and Annie took the sides. They pressed down and the tire began to rise.

"Go!" Naomi hollered.

The tire spun and caught traction. The station wagon grunted, then rolled forward. Twig brought the car to a quick stop, jumped out, and ran for Naomi. He wrapped his small arms around her waist.

"You're an answer to a prayer, Miss Naomi," he cried, "and I say a lot of 'em."

Naomi unwrapped the little boy from her waistline. Relieved tears rolled down his face and a wet spot spread across his pants.

"I'm pretty sure I know where I'm going," Mr. Mackey said, breaking the uncomfortable silence. "You're on River Street, right?"

"Yes, sir, number nineteen, on the left, but you can let me off at Manny's. It's where the bus stops. I can walk from there."

"Oh, no, I'll take you all the way home. River's off Magnolia, right?"

"Yes, sir." Naomi wondered how in the world this man knew her neighborhood so well.

Mr. Mackey turned the car onto Magnolia Street, where there were no magnolias, but a string of seedy establishments. It was an embarrassment, these places. Pappy's Wine and Spirits, with a sign that said MAD DOG 20/20 ON SALE; the Top Hat Club, which regularly collected a group of questionable characters out front; and the Drop 'N Go Cleaners, which had been closed for years.

Then Mr. Mackey turned onto River Street. The scenery improved only slightly, shotgun houses in various states of disrepair poised between the unpaved street and the wide, languid Congaree River.

"I always thought this would be a beautiful place to live," Mr. Mackey said, startling Naomi.

"Sir?"

"I think this is a pretty place; the river really is magnificent."

"You think the Bottom is *pretty?*"

"The geography certainly is. Certainly more interesting than Shimmering Pines, don't you think?"

All Naomi thought was she'd better keep her mouth shut. Lily's advice flashed like a warning light. *You gots to be careful on agreeing or disagreeing with any opinion white folks got 'cause soon as you do, they change they minds and you left stuck on the wrong side of that opinion.*

Mr. Mackey pulled up to her house, came to a stop, and put the Buick in park.

"Everything OK with Annie?"

"Just fine."

She had not told Mr. Mackey about the stuck car, about how Annie, Buck, and Twig had accompanied Briddy to a hamburger joint on Forest Drive where they each had a ten-cent burger. She had decided she would give the children—certainly Annie—this one chance. It was something her Grandee would've done. Among other things, Grandee was always good at not forgetting what it was like to be a child with nothing better to do than something you shouldn't do.

"Well, I sure appreciate you taking care of her."

"She's a nice child."

Mr. Mackey cleared his throat. He looked at Naomi's house.

"You've got a charming place," he said.

It was charming. After she and Luke were married, they had hoped to buy a house somewhere besides the Bottom. Standish Heights. Or Elmwood. Anywhere but the Bottom. But they had wound up with no other choice. Financially or otherwise. The Bottom was the only neighborhood in Columbia that realtors advertised as selling to COLORED in big, bold letters in the classified section of the newspaper. When Naomi first saw the clapboard house—grown gray and grim from years of no paint—she cried. But Luke persisted. He said it had a sound foundation and the plumbing was good. He promised to make it special. And that's exactly what he did. Whatever time Luke had between plumbing jobs was spent fixing the front steps, painting shutters, building window boxes. Nineteen River Street was a teal color, with creamy white shutters. It had a yellow door and preened like a lone, blooming wildflower in the winter woods.

Naomi reached for the door handle.

"Naomi?"

"Yes, sir?"

"I, well, before you go, I have a favor to ask of you."

"Yes, sir?"

"Well, if ever there was a bad time for me to be out of town, it's now, what with Mrs. Mackey in

Maryland and Annie getting ready to go back to school. But I've been invited to work with a group of graduate students in the historical restoration department at the College of Charleston. On the coast."

"I know where Charleston is."

"Of course you do. I'm sorry. Anyway, I've always wanted to try my hand at teaching, and given the subject matter—historical restoration—it's a great opportunity for me."

Naomi looked out the passenger window. How many opportunities had she had in her lifetime? None.

"I've talked to Mrs. Mackey's doctors, and they believe she will be in the hospital until the end of the year, at least. I haven't told Annie that, but the work in Charleston would be for the fall semester, so I would be in and out of town, for several days at a time, until Christmas. It's a seminar-type class, so it doesn't meet every day. My firm is all for it. I just don't know if you could…"

Again, Naomi remembered Lily's advice; she kept her silence.

Mr. Mackey rubbed his brow.

"Well, I wondered if you would be willing to stay with Annie at the house while I'm gone? Around the clock, I mean. I thought about asking her grandparents to come and take care of her, but they're pretty old. I think they would wear out with it, and I need someone I can count on."

Naomi took a deep breath, hoping it was loud enough for Mr. Mackey to hear.

"I'll have to think about it," she said. "I've made some commitments this fall and I'll have to see what I can do about that."

"I certainly understand. It's a lot to ask, but one way or the other, do you think you could let me know by the end of the week?"

"Yes, sir, I think I can."

"Well, I appreciate that. And there's one other thing. The doctors seem to think Mrs. Mackey will be well enough to see Annie by Thanksgiving. If that's the case, we'll be gone that week. You won't have to fool with us. It may be just as well not to be home..."

Mr. Mackey hesitated, staring at several children playing in the street. One was a tall, lithe boy, bouncing a basketball.

"Jesus, Will was such a beautiful young man. It's a terrible and inexplicable thing—losing a child. It feels like a chunk of my heart has been cut out."

"It'll start to fill back in one day," Naomi said.

"You think?"

The Lily warning light flashed again, but this time Naomi ignored it. She stared out the car window. She remembered Luke polishing the brass numbers one and nine he'd just screwed on the front door. They were so smart-looking.

She remembered how Luke stood back to study his handiwork. He was so proud.

"Naomi? You were saying?"

"Yes, it will fill back in one day, but not with the same material. Not nearly as strong. You'll have to take care with it."

"You're a smart lady, Naomi. I shouldn't be spilling my guts to you, but I thank you for listening all the same."

"You're welcome."

"And I'm sorry about your husband. What was his name?"

"Luke."

"Luke. Such a solid name."

"Yes," Annie said, "a solid name."

Naomi got out of the car, but turned back. Never mind Lily. The man needed her help.

"Mr. Mackey, I'll do whatever you need me to do this fall."

"But what about your other commitments?"

"I'll work around them," Naomi said, pushing the car door shut.

Mr. Mackey pulled away from the curb, found a place to turn around, and drove back past the teal cottage. The children playing in the street ran alongside the Buick as it went by. A nice car in the Bottom was a curiosity. So was a white man. Mr. Mackey waved to the children and they waved back.

It had been a long day and Naomi was glad to be home. Lily would surely come over in a few minutes to say hello. Naomi climbed the steps, made a mental note to water the geraniums, and pulled the screen door open. She was careful not to let it slam behind her. She hated slamming doors. The last thing she remembered about her daddy was the way he slammed the door when he left for good.

Naomi put her pocketbook down, walked into the small kitchen, and opened the refrigerator. There wasn't much there. She hadn't been hungry since Luke died. She closed the refrigerator door, poured a glass of water from the tap, and went out to the porch.

She sat in the swing. It had been a surprise from Luke. He had carved their names in the top slat. LUKE + NAOMI. He'd hung the swing one morning while she was at school. It always comforted her. Its back-and-forth motion and its rhythmic squeaks helped her sort things out.

She wondered about these white children who were slowly working their way into her heart. How she, Buck, Annie, and Twig had sat at the kitchen table and eaten cold fried chicken and talked about not getting in cars with unlicensed drivers anymore.

Twig had grasped a drumstick and asked her if she would wash his sheets for him. "And my pants, too. I wet 'em and our washing machine's broke and I don't want Mama having to do it. She gets mad."

"Real mad," Buck muttered.

Naomi remembered her own years of bedwetting. It began when she was four, maybe five. It began when the fights between her mother and father turned from words to fists.

So of course she told Twig she would wash his sheets, and his pants. But what she didn't tell him, in front of Buck and Annie, was that she would also help him quit soiling them. Grandee had taught her how not to; she would teach Twig. But it would be between the two of them. She would not tell Lily about Twig. And she certainly wouldn't tell Lily about the conversation she had with Annie after Buck and Twig had gone home.

"There's something else I need to tell you," Annie said, quietly. "When we were at Bell's, Briddy wouldn't let us sit with her. She said somebody was coming to see her. So we sat in another booth—me and Twig and Buck. Then a colored boy came in and he sat down with Briddy. Some man came over and told Briddy that the boy couldn't be there 'cause he was a ni—, um, you know, colored."

Naomi winced. "What did Briddy do?"

"She stood up, and the man wouldn't move out of the way and she sorta pushed him, and then she told us all to come on, we were leaving."

"Did you leave?"

"Uh-huh."

"What about the boy? The one who sat with Briddy?"

"He told Briddy not to worry about it. He left too. But not with us. In another car. I mean, he ain't—isn't—real colored, but kind of light brown. Kinda a funny color, actually. You know what I mean?"

Naomi knew what she meant. A mix. A mulatto. Maybe a quadroon. In any case, worse than being white and worse than being colored. No place to call home.

"Who is this boy?" Naomi asked.

"Briddy told us not to tell, but, well, he's in the symphonic band with her at school. She goes to Saint Timothy's, the Catholic school. She said they're letting a colored boy in this year. They've been having summer band practice, and Briddy met him there. His name is Terrence. And Naomi?"

"Yes?"

"Briddy says she likes him a whole lot. She says she don't care what color he is."

"*Doesn't.*"

"But shouldn't she care? I mean, it ain't—isn't—right, is it?"

"Lord, child, how would I know? My Grandee always says nothing good ever comes of white and colored folks mixing too much. But there again, we're all God's children, aren't we?"

"Well, we mix good, don't we? I mean, you and me?"

Naomi almost corrected Annie. *Well*, not good. But she decided against it.

"I suppose we do."

"Naomi?"

"Yes?"

"I miss my mama. I miss her real bad."

Naomi reached for Annie. The child crawled into her lap and began to cry. Naomi held her close. The top of Annie's head, tucked underneath Naomi's chin, smelled like woods and fresh air. Naomi began to rock, back and forth, and she hummed a quiet song. Just as Grandee did with her. Just as she would have done with her own child.

Naomi picked a piece of grass out of Annie's hair. Then she studied Annie's hands. The fingernails were short and ragged. The cuticles were dry and cracked.

"When are you going to start taking care of these fingernails?" Naomi asked Annie, spreading the child's hands out in the palms of her own.

Annie lifted her head off Naomi's chest and inspected her hands.

"I don't know. Are they bad?"

"Well, one of these days, you know, you're going to be a young lady and you'll want pretty hands and fingernails."

"You think?"

"Think what?"

"That some day I'll be a lady? I mean, instead of a girl?"

"I'm sure of it," Naomi said.

"But I'm not sure I want to be one. Sounds boring."

"Oh, no," Naomi said, "just a little different. Now, if I give you some Vaseline, will you rub it into your cuticles every night? That will soften the skin and keep your cuticles from cracking and you from picking at them."

"I reckon."

"You reckon?"

"No, I promise."

"Now that's better," Naomi said, wrapping a hand around Annie's head and pulling it back against her shoulder. It was a comfort, having the child rest against her. Naomi felt full, in a way only a child's weight in her lap could fill her.

"Hey, Naomi?"

"Hmm?"

"Thanks a bunch for helping us today."

"You're most welcome, but please don't do something so dangerous again. Your daddy would have a fit."

"You ain't gonna tell him, are you?"

"Only if you'll say *aren't* instead of ain't."

"Aren't," Annie said, resting her head back against Naomi's shoulder.

CHAPTER FIVE

nnie stirred in her sleeping bag. She opened her eyes and looked into the canopy of the Old Lady. Branches emerged inky black against the night sky, like a giant spider web. A glimmer of tawny light shimmered in the distance. Heat lightning. Amiable rumbles of thunder wandered across the fields below the bluff.

Annie turned in her sleeping bag, tucked her arms under her pillow, and wondered if anyone else was awake. She, Buck, and Twig were camping out. It was Last Camp, the night they spent in sleeping bags under the Old Lady at the end of every summer. Always a Saturday night before school started the next week. They celebrated the evening with A&W root beer and lemon coolers.

The only thing different about this year's Last Camp was Briddy's absence. She had announced she was too old for it; she wanted to watch her favorite television show, *Dr. Kildare.*

Annie's sleeping bag was a heavy green affair that smelled like mothballs. Her mama put mothballs in everything. Annie had finally gotten a letter from her. It came in a pale pink envelope with matching stationery inside.

Dear Annie,

I hope you are doing well. I am feeling better. The doctors and nurses here are very nice. It is a beautiful place. The food is good—maybe too good—and I take a walk every afternoon. It is not nearly as hot as I'm sure it is in Columbia. I am sorry I will not be home when you begin junior high. You are growing up so fast. I miss you.

Love,

Mama

Her mother's writing looked careful, controlled. The letter sounded like a second grader had written it. Or someone who *had* to write something, but didn't *want* to write something.

"Well, I miss you too," Annie had grumbled, folding it up and stashing it in the drawer of her bedside table. Something about the letter made her mad, and she decided not to write back until Naomi insisted that it would be the right thing to do.

"You remember how hard your mama is trying to get around that truck. And you write her back."

"But she doesn't sound like she cares if I write her back or not."

"She may not sound like it, but she does."

So Annie had taken out pen and paper.

Dear Mama,

Thanks for your letter. It was not very long, but that's OK. Naomi said you might not have much time to write. Naomi is the colored lady working here now. I like her better than Ruth. (Remember Ruth? She didn't like the Ouija board.) Sometimes Naomi spends the night when Daddy is teaching in Charleston. Did you know he was doing that? He said it is very interesting what he is doing which is teaching about fixing old buildings. I like Naomi a lot. The only thing is she is always telling me how to talk. We watched Martin Luther King on TV when he was in Washington giving the dream speech. It was kind of cool. Did you see all those people? Naomi says he is a very smart man. What do you think? Buck is doing good. He said to tell you hi. (Hi!)

Twig is doing good to. I think Briddy has a boy-friend. He is going to Saint Tim's. He is not all white or all colored. Naomi said he is something in the middle. I don't think anybody but me, Buck, and Twig know about it. And Naomi. Oh, well. When are you coming home? I miss you and I am glad you feel better.

Love, Annie

P.S. Buck misses your brownies.

P.S.S. Naomi told me a judge in Columbia decided colored people should be able to go to Sesqui Park and swim in the lake. Remember when we used to take walks out at Sesqui on Sunday afternoons? That was fun. Naomi said they are going to close the park for Labor Day so colored people can't come. I thought you had to do what a judge says. Me and Naomi were talking about that after watching the dream speech. It has to do with people being equal and getting to do the same things and all that.

P.S.S.S. I am a little nervous about going to junior high. And by the way, Daddy got me a transistor radio. I listen to Woody with the Goodies every night on WCOS before I go to sleep. My favorite song right now is "Surf City." Have you heard it?

P.S.S.S.S. No more P.S.s!

Far more insistent lightning spread across the sky, followed by thunderclaps. Buck turned over in his sleeping bag. Ugly began to whine. He hated storms.

"It's OK," Annie told the dog, stroking his rough fur. Ugly crawled over to Annie on his belly and buried his head in her neck. His nose was wet and cold.

"Hey," Annie asked Buck, poking him in the side, "you awake?"

"Yeah. What time is it?"

"Dunno. Late."

"Is it gonna storm?"

"Ugly sure thinks so. Daddy says dogs know before people do when a storm is coming."

"Hey, Annie?" Buck rolled over onto his back. He cupped his hands under his head.

"Huh?"

"I've been meaning to ask you something."

"Ask away."

"It's about school. I mean, you'll be at Crayton with me this year."

"So?"

"Well, it's different there. You know, more kids and everything."

"I know."

"So, you're not gonna go getting a boyfriend, are you?"

Annie felt her stomach catch.

"What do you care?"

"Well, I reckon I care some. I don't want you to go messing around with some stupid boy or something. I mean, we've always kind of been a pair, right?"

"I guess so."

"You guess so?"

"Well, it's not like we're girl- and boyfriend. I mean, what if I meet a cute boy? Are you gonna go getting mad or something?"

Buck lay back down in his sleeping bag. He crossed his arms over his eyes. "Never mind."

"Hey, what're y'all doing?" Twig asked. He was curled up like a snail inside a shell on the other side of Annie. Twig never brought a sleeping bag, just an armful of old blankets. It was easier to wash one or two blankets than a fat sleeping bag.

"Just talking," Buck said.

Annie smiled to herself.

A blaze of white lightning flashed through the Old Lady. A clap of thunder shook the ground underneath them.

"Hey, y'all, I think we better get out of here," Annie said.

"Wanna go to the barn?" Buck asked.

"Shoot, no," Twig said, "that place gives me the creeps. We got time to get home, but we should pray first."

"For what?" Annie asked. "For lightning not to hit us crossing First Field?"

"Exactly. Saint Thomas Aquinas helps keep folks from getting struck by..."

"I'm just getting my stuff and getting out of here," Buck grumbled. "Com'on, Annie."

Twig crossed himself.

Lightning lit the flat expanse of First Field like stadium lights. Annie ran hard. She could feel electricity in the night air. The hair on her arms stood up. Her daddy once told her if she felt that, the lightning was real close. Maybe they should have prayed.

"Hurry, y'all!" Buck hollered over his shoulder. Annie ran faster. She could hear Twig behind her, running hard, too.

By the time they reached the barbed wire fence, the sky had opened up. One of Twig's blankets got hung up in the fence. "Wait," he screamed, "I gotta get it."

"No, you don't," Buck hollered back, "now com'on!"

They made it to Annie's house and dropped their soaked belongings in the carport.

"Y'all just wanna stay here?" Annie hollered above the noise of the rain. It was coming down sideways now. She hoped Buck would say yes.

"Hey y'all, what's that?" Twig asked. He'd wandered over to the front of the carport. He stood still, looking toward his house.

"What's what?" Buck said.

"I don't know. Something blue. Jumping around. See it?"

Buck and Annie walked over to the edge of the carport, and sure enough, a blue, frenzied light bounced through the rain from the direction of the Roebuck house.

"What is *that*?" Twig stammered.

"That's a dadgum police car!" Buck responded.

Twig dropped his other wet blanket, crossed himself, and took off through the rain. When he wanted to run fast, there was no catching him. Buck and Annie chased him through the storm, but by the time they reached the Roebuck house, Twig had already slammed the front door behind him.

Annie sucked in heavy, wet air. She stared at the front door. The doorbell gleamed like a miniature full moon. She did not dare touch it. Inside, she could hear Mrs. Roebuck screaming.

"What do you see?" Annie asked.

Buck was hanging off the brick ledge of a window next to the door; his bare toes dug into the crevices of the brick for purchase.

"A real fat cop," he said. "He's got his thumbs hooked in his belt. Mrs. Roebuck's in her durn nightie. She's got pink rollers in her hair. She's hollering at the cop. Twig's on his knees, praying."

"What about Mr. Roebuck?"

"Don't see him."

"Briddy?"

"Nope."

"What do you reckon's going on?"

"Search me," Buck said, lowering himself from the window.

"You didn't hear any words?" Annie asked.

"Just screaming, but nothing I could make out."

"Bet Briddy did something."

"Like what?"

"Like I don't know, but something. She's been acting so funny lately."

Ugly whimpered.

"Well, we sure ain't going in there, so I reckon we oughta go home," Buck said.

Annie and Buck walked down the street. The rain had slowed, but water washed across the asphalt in shallow waves.

"Wanna stay at my house?" Annie asked Buck.

"Naw, I better get on home."

"Well, how come...?"

"Listen, Annie, it ain't got nothing to do with what we talked about under the Old Lady. I just, well, I just feel like I need to get on home. I don't know, something don't feel right."

"Like what?"

Buck was quiet.

"Like what?" Annie asked again.

"Like I gotta look after Dad in the morning. Eunice is on vacation and Mama's working a double shift at the hospital and I gotta help him get his shower and stuff. Jack won't do it."

Buck's father, Bill, was a retired army drill sergeant who spent most of his time in a wheelchair after suffering a broken back while training recruits at Fort Jackson, the big army base in Columbia. Buck's mother was a quiet, thoughtful woman named Marie who was a nurse at Baptist Memorial Hospital downtown. Annie loved to hear her stories of babies being born, but she didn't love being around Buck's big brother, Jack, who was mean as a snake. Especially to Buck.

Annie and Buck reached the Mackey carport and Buck grabbed his sleeping bag. Annie stood on the concrete steps leading to the side door, watching him.

"Well, then," Buck said, "I reckon I'll see you tomorrow some time. Wanna go fishing? We haven't done that in a while."

"Sure," Annie said. "What time?"

"Two o'clock? Meet at the Old Lady?"

"OK, see you then."

Annie watched Buck walk out of the carport into the rain. Ugly followed right behind him. The pair went up the street and turned a corner toward the McCain house.

Upstairs, Annie passed by her mother and father's bedroom door. The light was on. Naomi was propped up, reading in the big bed.

"Is that you?" Naomi asked.

"Yeah, it started to storm."

"Well, I'm glad you're in. I was beginning to worry. Make sure you put your wet things in the dirty basket. Sleep tight and say your prayers."

"Naomi?"

"Yes?"

"Can I ask you something?"

"Certainly, but get some dry things on first. I don't want you catching cold right before school starts."

Annie returned to her parents' bedroom in one of Will's old T-shirts.

"Can I get in?"

"Sure," Naomi said, patting the bed.

Annie crawled in the big bed. It felt warm and soft.

"Now, what's on your mind?" Naomi said, putting her book on the bedside table.

"Do you think Buck likes me?"

"I'm sure he does. You two have been friends for a long time, haven't you?"

"I mean like a girlfriend."

"Now, I don't know about that, but what makes you wonder?"

"He said he didn't want me getting a boyfriend when I got to Crayton. He said we were a pair."

"Hmm. Well, you're too young for a boy-friend, but it sounds like Buck may be a little worried."

"About what?"

"Well, sharing you. You're pretty, and you're cute, and now you're going to junior high school. It's a big change for you and Buck."

"How so?"

"Well, in a way, Buck is used to having you—your friendship—all to himself. With Twig and Briddy, too, but mainly you. What makes it different is now you'll be making new friends, and more friends, at Crayton. I suspect that concerns him a little. He doesn't want you to forget about him. He doesn't want things to change between the two of you."

"It won't."

Naomi held Annie's hand.

"But it probably will, baby. Things always change. Just keep in mind that Buck is sensitive to it and you two will be fine."

Annie pulled at a loose thread in the chenille bedspread.

"Don't mess with that," Naomi admonished. "I need to fix it."

"Naomi?"

"Hmm?"

"There was a police car at the Roebucks' when we got back from the farm."

"A police car? Are you sure?"

"Yep. Buck and I tried to figure out what was going on. A big cop was talking to Mrs. Roebuck, but we couldn't tell."

"Goodness. Well, I hope everything is OK."

"You think it's about that colored boy? That's what I think."

"Lord, I hope not, but I think you and I need to go to bed."

Naomi reached for the bedside light.

"Can I sleep with you?" Annie asked.

"I would love that."

Annie buried deep in the covers. Naomi turned off the light and closed her eyes.

Naomi was six years old when her father had left for good. Her harried mama took her to the country—to Grandee's neatly kept cabin on several acres of just as carefully kept land near the town of McCormick.

"I don't know what to do with her," Naomi's mama had said to Grandee. "I've got to keep my job at the Laundromat."

"Let her stay with me, at least for the summer," Grandee said.

That night, after a warm supper of grits and biscuits, Grandee took Naomi's hand and walked her into the small bedroom at the back of the cabin. A double bed filled the room. Grandee patted the mattress, made of corn shucks and blue-striped ticking.

"It might feel funny at first, but you'll get used to it," Grandee said, tucking Naomi in. "I'll be in later, after I finish my reading."

Naomi clutched the edge of the patchwork quilt under her chin. "I miss my mama," she said.

"I know you do, baby, but you're gonna be just fine. You'll see. Now, say your prayers and ask God for a bluebird sky tomorrow."

"A bluebird sky?"

"A sky so clear and blue we'll have all day to do all the things we need to do and all the things we want to do."

CHAPTER SIX

Naomi loved to fish. When she stayed with her Grandee in the summer, they would fish in the early evenings, in a small pond Grandee called "the puddle." It was an easy walk to the puddle along a sandy path that began at the back stoop of Grandee's cabin. The path twinkled with tiny bits of broken mica. Grandee called it "ground gold." When they reached the puddle, Grandee sat by the edge of the water on a slat-back chair she kept propped against a pine tree. Naomi sat on an upturned bucket until she or Grandee caught a fish, then she sat on the ground.

Before they departed for the puddle, Naomi dug for worms in the ebony loam of the vegetable garden. The worms were long and fat. Naomi found them easily—always careful to pull them out of the earth in one piece. She closed her fist around them; they wiggled in her hand with a ferocity that always surprised her. She felt guilty dropping them into the blue coffee can, but Grandee called it "the reason of life."

"We all here for a reason of life and the reason for these worms is some fine, fine fishing," Grandee would proclaim, inspecting Naomi's findings.

So when Annie announced Sunday afternoon that she and Buck were going fishing at the pond on the farm, Naomi couldn't resist.

"There's a fishing pond?" she asked, finishing the dishes.

"Yep. Looks like a bowl of pea soup, but it's got some big fish in it."

"I haven't gone fishing in a long time," Naomi ruminated, wiping her hands on her apron.

"You like to fish?"

"Oh, child, I love to. Grandee always took me fishing if we got our work done. Right at dusk, when it wasn't dark but it wasn't light either. There was something about that time of day that was so peaceful. Watching that bobber sitting on top of the water, waiting for it to jiggle. It teaches you patience like nothing else I know of. And when that bobber finally shot under the water, well, it was just so quick, so fast! Like a spell had been broken. Lord, yes, I *love* to fish."

"Well, Buck always brings extra poles. A while back, he said he wanted you to see the farm, so why don't you come with us? Maybe Twig'll show up and we can find out what happened at the Roebucks' last night."

When Naomi had driven Annie to Sunday school, they had passed by the Roebuck house. There were no lights on. The den curtains were pulled closed. The garage door was down.

"Well," Naomi said, "if Twig brings it up, that's one thing, but we shouldn't pry."

"Pry?"

"Ask questions. Poke around."

"You know a lot of funny words."

"Grandee used to sit me down every night during the summertime. At the kitchen table. I'd have to open the dictionary—seemed like the size of a suitcase—and I'd have to close my eyes and put my finger on a word. If she thought the word was hard enough, or she didn't know it, then I'd have to learn it."

"What if the word wasn't hard enough?"

"I'd have to put my finger on another one. Now, are you ready to go? I know I am."

Naomi looked forward to her first venture across the barbed wire fence, but she did not expect to be so mesmerized by the farm. Its wide, open spaces were such a change from the restrained feeling of Shimmering Pines. Fields spread out like milk spills. Burly oaks, sturdy hickories, tall pines, and the occasional clutch of wild dogwoods bordered the fields with casual gracefulness. Nothing like the fenced backyards in Shimmering Pines. Or the rows of orderly shrubs separating one front yard from another.

"My goodness," Naomi said, halfway across First Field, following Annie, Buck, and Ugly along the deer path.

"Ain't it beautiful out here?" Buck said. Over his shoulder he carried three cane poles and a bright green rod with a Zebco reel.

"It certainly is, *isn't* it?"

"You haven't seen anything yet," Annie said, carrying a folding chair for Naomi. "Wait 'til you see the Old Lady up close. She's something else."

The live oak stood in the distance. As Naomi got closer to the tree, she could see what Annie was talking about. It was a miracle of sorts, its size enough to take a person's breath away. Spanish moss decorated the Old Lady's limbs like she was dressed for a dance. And those magnificent limbs. Their girths were testimony to strength and time. Not the human variety, but the Lord's kind. Power and might. A world without end.

Twig was nestled in his favorite branch. "Hey, there," he called out.

"Hey back," Buck said. "We're going fishing. Naomi's coming too. Wanna go?"

"Sure," Twig said, scrambling down to the ground.

"How're you today?" he said to Naomi, extending his right hand.

"Just fine," she said, enveloping his delicate hand in her own. "But I thought you would be bringing me some sheets to wash."

"Mama got the washing machine fixed."

"Well, that's good, but I want to talk to you sometime."

"About what?"

Naomi leaned over and whispered in Twig's ear. "It's a secret; you come see me after school one day, OK?"

"OK!" Twig beamed.

When Grandee had taught Naomi how not to wet her bed, it had been a project that was a secret pact between the two of them. "No need for anybody to know about this but you and me," Grandee had said. "Some things need to stay 'tween two people. Not any more."

Naomi meant for it to be that way between her and Twig.

Buck, Annie, Twig, and Naomi traveled over the far end of the bluff and down a narrow path etched into the side of the hill.

"Careful," Buck said to Naomi, "it's slick as owl shit going down here."

The group crossed another field—not nearly as impressive as First Field—and arrived at the pond, a pool of green, murky water surrounded by a bank carpeted in goldenrod and Queen Anne's lace. Several turtles were sunning themselves on the end of a fallen tree. When the somber creatures heard the commotion of human visitors, they slipped quietly off the log and into the water. Circles rippled out from their entry point.

A dock that had surely seen better days extended out into the water from the far side of the bank. Rusted nails poked up out of the warped planks.

Annie, Buck, and Twig settled themselves on the dock. Naomi sat in her folding chair.

"Want me to bait your hook?" Buck asked Naomi. He was reaching into a Chase & Sanborn coffee can. It was funny how some things never changed, Naomi thought. Like worms in coffee cans.

"Why, thank you," Naomi said, extending the end of her cane pole to Buck.

Buck wrapped a fat worm around the hook. "Now," he said, wiping his hands on his shorts, "see if you can get your hook in them cattails over there. There's a big old bass that hangs out in 'em. We call him Butthead. It's 'bout time he got caught."

Naomi made one easy swing of her cane pole and landed her hook and bobber in the cattails.

"Perfect," Buck said, impressed.

"Hey, Twig," Annie asked, "how's everything going?"

Naomi cleared her throat; Annie persisted. "I mean, you OK after last night and all?"

Annie was lying on the warm dock, the tip of her cane pole resting between her toes. She didn't care if she caught any fish or not. She just liked being here. And she wanted to know what had happened at the Roebucks'.

"Briddy's grounded and can't go nowhere, 'cept school. She can't get her driver's license either."

"What'd Briddy do?" Annie asked.

Naomi shifted in her chair and gave Annie a stern look.

Annie shrugged. "I mean, you don't have to tell me if you don't want."

"Well, as a matter of fact, it's all right here in the newspaper," Twig said, reaching into his pants pocket and pulling out a carefully folded piece of paper.

"The newspaper?" Buck said, turning his attention away from his bobber, which also floated in the cattails.

"Yep, Briddy made the paper," Twig said.

Naomi felt uncomfortable. Grandee always said there were only two times people should be in the newspaper—when they got married and when they died. Colored folks, she added, only got in when they died. White or colored, anything else most likely meant trouble.

"Want me to read the article?" Twig asked.

"Sure," Annie said.

Twig cleared his throat and read:

A Columbia youth was arrested Saturday night and charged in connection with an incident in which a Negro youth received an eye injury. The incident occurred at 9:20 p.m. at Gene's Pig 'n Chick Drive-In on Devine Street when Terrence Roberts, 17,

**of 165 Standish Street, was reportedly hit
in the face while trying to 'stand up' for his
girlfriend, who is white.**

"That's Briddy," Twig explained. "You know,
the girlfriend."

Naomi's stomach turned a notch.

"We know," Buck said.

"Well, maybe Naomi don't."

"Keep reading," Buck grumbled.

Twig continued:

**Richland County Deputy J. P. Bole said the
white youth, 17-year-old Thomas Walburn
of 135 Spring Lake Road, was arrested
on North Trenholm Road at 11:30 p.m.
Saturday by Deputies Bole and Randall
McDowell. "Walburn made an insulting
remark to Roberts's girlfriend," Deputy Bole
said, "and when Roberts asked Walburn to**

apologize for the remark, Walburn hit him in the face."

"Now listen to *this*," Twig said. He read:

Roberts is the son of Sylvia and Matthew Roberts, who recently became the first Negro to be hired by the federal Internal Revenue Service office in Columbia. The Roberts family moved to Columbia from New Jersey in June. Terrence is set to be the first colored student to attend St. Timothy's Catholic School, a parochial school in Columbia. Classes begin Tuesday. When reached at home, Mr. Roberts, Terrence's father, said he would not comment on the incident at the drive-in or his son's upcoming attendance at a previously all-white school.

"Bet he can't wait to get out of a colored school," Buck said.

"But don't you think it'd be kind of weird having a colored kid in a white school?" Annie asked.

Naomi turned in her chair. "Do you think it would be weird going to school with me?"

"Well, sure. You're too old."

"What Naomi means is she's colored and you're white and you like her so what's the big deal?" Twig said.

"How do you know what I mean?" Naomi asked Twig.

"Well, I don't know. I mean, I *reckon* that's what you meant."

"*Hey, Naomi!*" Buck hollered, jumping to his feet. "*You got a bite! A big one!*"

Naomi looked into the brown cattails for her bobber and saw nothing. A strong yank jerked her fishing line out of the cattails and into the middle of the pond. Naomi stood up from her chair, her cane pole bending to the point of breaking.

"Holy shit!" Buck hollered. *"It's him! It's Butthead! Goddern, Naomi, you got that sucker!"*

"I'm not going to have him long," Naomi grimaced, wrestling with the pole. "He's bound to break this..."

The pole snapped in half. Naomi held the fat end while the skinny piece zigzagged through the water.

"No darn way!" Buck cried, diving into the pond. He swam furiously and reached for the end of the pole. Once in hand, he dragged it back to Naomi, who pulled the line in. She couldn't imagine how much the fish weighed. Ten pounds? More?

The glistening bass broke the surface of the water, its mouth a gaping, pink hole big enough to put a fist in. Buck scrambled onto the dock and grabbed the fish's mouth. He pulled it onto the dock where it lay, gulping for air.

Everyone stood over the fish except Twig, who sank to his knees, clasping his hands together. "Please, Saint Andrew, let the hook come out easy."

"Saint Andrew?" Naomi asked.

"Patron saint of fishermen. He'll help Buck get that hook out."

"Hook ain't bad," Buck said, reaching into the fish's mouth with needle-nose pliers.

Twig crossed himself.

"I think we should return him to the water," Naomi announced.

"Are you kidding?" Buck cried, his eyes widening in disbelief. "You could get this thing stuffed. You could get a picture in the paper of this thing."

"I'm not kidding at all. It's my fish. And he belongs in the water."

"That's the craziest thing I ever heard of," Buck said, disgusted. "We been trying to catch him for years."

"It's not any more crazy than anything else," Naomi said. "Why, do you think that colored boy—what's his name? Terrence?—do you think he likes being jerked out of his old school up there in New Jersey where he's likely comfortable and happy to be put in another one where it's not going to be nearly so comfortable and happy?"

Buck stared at Naomi. So did Twig and Annie.

"Well, do you?" Naomi repeated. "Do you really think he is going to be happier in a school full of white children who think something's wrong with him because he's another color?"

"Maybe they won't think anything's wrong with him," Twig mumbled. "Briddy don't."

"Briddy *doesn't,* and that makes her mighty special in my book, but I can guarantee you everybody else does."

Buck picked the big fish up carefully and gently lowered it into the water. The fish floated on its side, not moving. "Goddern it." Buck reached in the water and pulled the fish backwards, filling its gills with water. "Now go on, git."

The creature came to life with a flash of green and silver and swam away.

"Thank you," Naomi said quietly, folding her chair. "I believe I will go home now."

Naomi walked off the dock and toward the bluff. Buck and Annie stared at one another, not sure what to think. Twig took off, hollering for Naomi to wait up.

She did not.

CHAPTER SEVEN

Twig caught up to Naomi by the time she reached the barbed wire fence.

"You mad about something?" he asked, holding the wire down to the ground for her.

"Yes," Naomi said, stepping over.

"Well, um, if it's about Terrence, you don't need to worry. I think Briddy'll be nice to him. She likes him a whole lot. I mean, it's not like he's real colored."

Naomi looked at Twig. He was so small. And so naïve. She chose her words carefully. "I am uncomfortable with this kind of talk."

"What kind of talk?"

"Colored talk. Colored this and colored that."

"But I told you, Terrence ain't all that colored and Briddy likes him."

"Let me tell you something. Terrence is a Negro. In the white man's book, it doesn't matter *how* colored, as you say, he is. He may be brown like the shell of a roasted peanut or he may be black as a witch's cat, but he is a Negro and nothing good will come of your sister liking him. Not for her and not for him. Now that's all I have to say about it."

Naomi continued her walk across the Mackeys' yard. She wanted to be alone, but Twig followed her, dragging his stick across the dirt. It made a scraping noise that dogged Naomi's nerves like a stray pup. She was glad to reach the back door of the Mackey house.

"Naomi?"

"*What now*?"

"Never mind," Twig murmured.

Twig looked like he'd been struck. His head drooped; his shoulders curled in like a fallen leaf.

"I'm sorry," Naomi said. "What is it?"

"You told me you wanted to talk about something. You said it was a secret."

Naomi opened the back door. "Come in, but leave that blessed stick outside."

Twig sat at the kitchen table while Naomi retrieved two Coca-Colas from the refrigerator. She popped the top off each thick, green bottle. Then she sat down across from Twig.

"First of all," she said, "I want you to understand this is between you and me."

"You mean the secret?"

"That's what I mean. Now, when I was a little girl, I started wetting my bed too. It seemed like it came out of nowhere, and every morning or so, I'd wake up and my sheets would be wet. My mama couldn't understand why I did it. All she would do is get mad at me, but she would never help me."

"My mama gets mad at me too. She thinks God is getting back at her for something. It's terrible."

"I know it is, child. I know it is. So, during the summer I went to the country to spend time with my grandmother. I called her Grandee. Now Grandee wasn't an educated woman."

"She didn't go to school?"

"Not much. But she was smart. And every night, I would spend the night in her bed with her because it was the only bed in her little place. I loved sleeping with her. Oh, how I loved it, but one night I wet the bed. I had a bad dream."

"About what?"

"My mama and daddy fighting."

"Did she get mad?"

"Grandee? Oh, no. She took the sheets off the bed, washed them in a bin, and strung them out on the line to dry. I will never forget those flowery sheets whipping in the wind. I pushed my face into them while they were still drying and they smelled wonderful. So fresh and sweet. Grandee was standing on the back stoop and called me to come in. I figured I was in trouble then. I held my head down. I was so embarrassed and—oh, I will never forget how gentle she was—she put her hand underneath my chin, raised my head up, and looked into my eyes. She told me there was nothing to be ashamed of and to sit in her lap.

"We sat there on that back stoop for the longest time, talking about things. My mama. My daddy leaving her. How sad and angry it made my mama. How hard my mama worked just to keep our heads above water. And then we talked about what makes a body wet the bed. I thought it would be an embarrassing conversation to have, but it wasn't. Just like I don't want this one to be. Are you embarrassed?"

"Not so far."

"Well, that's good. So, Grandee said there can be lots of reasons why someone like you and me wet the bed when we're young. One reason is a little person's bladder is just too small to handle all the yellow water his body makes."

"Yellow water?"

"That's what Grandee called it, but urine, if you prefer."

"Oh, OK. Pee. So, you think my bladder is too small?"

"I think it's a possibility, especially since you're so small yourself. Now tell me, do you drink a lot of liquid before you go to bed at night?"

"Well, Mama always keeps a pitcher of sweet tea in the refrigerator. I drink a lot of that. But I ain't never thought about *when* I drink it."

"Well, don't drink any of it past five o'clock in the afternoon, and do your best not to drink much of anything else after that time either. If you get thirsty, swish water around in your mouth, but try not to drink it. Can you do that?"

"I sure can."

"OK, that's the first part of the plan. The second part is a little more complicated."

"How so?"

Naomi's eyes sparkled. "We're going to do something not many people know how to do. We're going to grow your bladder."

Twig put his Coca-Cola bottle on the table and stared at Naomi.

"We're gonna *what?*"

"We're going to make your bladder expand itself so that it can hold more for longer periods of time. That way, when your bladder is finished expanding, it can hold your yellow water all night long."

"Well, how do we do that?"

"We make up a schedule for you. Every day, you're going to drink more water than the day before. And every day, you're going to hold off going to the bathroom for a few more minutes than you did the day before. Think about an athlete running a little farther and a little longer every day. One day he'll be able to run a long, long way. Does that make sense?"

"Sure does. When can I start?"

"As soon as you want to."

"How about right now?"

"Fine," Naomi said. She went to the kitchen sink and poured Twig a big glass of cool tap water. She returned to the table and set the glass in front of him. While he drank the water, Naomi made up a calendar of days, amounts of water, and times to pee, and put it all on paper.

"How long's this gonna take?" Twig asked, looking at the schedule.

"No more than a month or two, if you stick to the schedule and don't tell anybody what you're doing."

"Why not?"

"Because somebody's likely to tell you it won't work and you'll get a bad idea in your head that it won't work and then it might not work. But I'm telling you, it *will* work. It worked for me, and it will work for you."

"Wow, thanks so much, Naomi."

"You're welcome, my little friend. Now here, come sit in my lap."

Twig didn't hesitate. He arranged himself in Naomi's lap. It was a good place to be.

"There's one more thing," Naomi said.

"What's that?"

"Well, when I started wetting the bed, I was going to bed with bad thoughts at night. I was scared about my mama and how she was acting. She was so angry about my daddy, and she would scream and take the Lord's name in vain. Sometimes she'd drink too much alcohol, and she even hit me one time. She didn't hit me too hard, mind you, but hard enough. I think I stayed scared a lot during that time, and I know I went to bed feeling sad and frightened. It made my stomach hurt a lot. Do you ever feel that way when you go to bed?"

Twig's head rested against Naomi's pillowy chest.

"Sometimes," he said quietly.

"Can you tell me why?"

"Daddy gets drunk and screams at Mama about the church. He says it's stupid how much time she spends there and she might as well be married to God as to him. She says Jesus wasn't the only immaculate concession."

"Con-*cep*-tion, but never mind, go on."

"Well, Mama cries when he does that, and then she starts screaming at me and Briddy."

"What about?"

"Anything. It don't matter, but lately, it's been mostly about Briddy. How she don't do what Mama says. How she got in that mess at the drive-in with Terrence. How she's supposed to stay a virgin, whatever that is, for a long, long time, and how she ain't supposed to be messing around with any boys, 'specially a nig...um, a colored boy."

147

"Were you going to say nigger?"

"I didn't mean to. I stopped it. I never want to hurt nobody."

"*Anybody*?"

"Anybody."

Naomi pulled Twig tighter to her chest.

"You know, Twig, I never had an opportunity to have children, but if I had, I would've wanted one just like you. There isn't a mean bone in your body, and you've got a lot of sense in your head. You're going to grow up to be a fine young man, do you know that?"

"You think so?"

"I know so. Now, about these feelings you have before you go to bed. You have to understand that you can't solve other people's problems. You can't fix how mad your mama and daddy get at each other. You can't fix the fact that

Briddy likes Terrence. All you can do is fix *you*. So here's what we're gonna do. Besides sticking to your schedule of drinking and making water during the day, you're going to eat a spoonful of honey every night before you go to bed. I'll get you the spoon and the honey. "

"What's that gonna do?"

"It's going to do the same thing it did for me. It's going to give you sweet, peaceful thoughts at night, instead of the other kind."

"Promise?"

"Promise. Now all this is between you and me, right?"

"You bet," Twig said, sitting up in Naomi's lap.

"You know, if this works, I'm gonna petition the Catholic church to make you the saint of clean sheets. I wanted to be that saint, but you'd be better."

"Well, don't you think Grandee deserves to be the saint of fresh sheets? After all, she's the one who came up with the plan."

"Yeah, I reckon so."

Naomi and Twig sat quietly at the kitchen table. Naomi began to rock back and forth, humming softly. Twig put his head back down against Naomi's chest.

"Naomi?"

"Hmm?"

"I'm sorry you ain't—haven't—got a kid. If I can ever get you one, I will. I swear I will."

"Now what'd I tell you about not trying to fix other folks' problems?"

"Not to try."

"That's right. Besides, I've got you, don't I?"

"Yep, you sure do."

CHAPTER EIGHT

Briddy's hair fell to the kitchen floor in long, thick clumps. Mrs. Roebuck wielded a weighty pair of scissors in her right hand. In her left, she grasped what was left of Briddy's ponytail. One more sharp whack and it was all gone.

Mrs. Roebuck stood still, her arms hanging by her side. She was breathing hard. Briddy turned around and looked at her mother.

"Are you happy now?" the girl asked, shorn of her beautiful tresses. What was left of Briddy's hair sprouted forth from her head like the occasional wild onion on a well-trimmed lawn.

"That fancy colored boy won't be, will he?" Mrs. Roebuck snapped.

Briddy stood her ground. "Terrence isn't fancy, whatever that means. And he doesn't care what I look like. He loves me."

"Loves you? All he wants is sex. All any boy wants is sex. Especially colored boys. But I doubt he'll want sex with you now. So, yes, I'm happy. And I'm going to church to pray for your soul. While I'm gone, make sure you clean up this mess."

Briddy waited until her mother had left the house to sweep her hair off the floor. She gathered it up and placed it in a small box lined with white tissue. She would keep the hair to remind her of this day forever. She would never forget what had just happened in the kitchen, and she would never forgive her mother for it. Never.

Briddy closed the box and secured it with small snips of tape. She pushed it underneath her bed, where no one would find it.

"Briddy?" It was Twig, at her bedroom door.

"What?"

"Can I come in?"

"You can do anything you want. I don't care."

Twig crept into Briddy's bedroom. He'd heard the commotion in the kitchen. When Briddy turned to look at him, his mouth fell open.

"What? Can't think of anything to say, little brother? How about 'Nice haircut'?"

"It's horrible. I mean, it's horrible what Mama did. I'm sorry."

Twig climbed onto Briddy's bed.

"Can I touch it?" he asked.

"Why?"

"I don't know. I just want to."

"Help yourself."

Briddy leaned forward. Cautiously, Twig moved his hand across the top of his sister's head.

"You want me to fix the spots? Smooth it out a little?"

"Sure. The scissors are still in the kitchen, on the countertop. Point 'em down coming back."

Twig returned from the kitchen with the scissors. He sat on his haunches on the bed. Briddy sat cross-legged in front of him. Twig began snipping longer bits of hair off his sister's head.

"Do you know what Robert Frost wrote about love?" Briddy asked her little brother.

"Who's Robert Frost?"

"A poet."

"No, what'd he write?"

"Love is the irresistible desire to be irresistibly desired."

"What does that mean?"

"I think it means a person can't help but want to be loved. I can't help but want to be loved by Terrence. I think he feels the same way. So, we love each other. Does that make sense?"

"But he's colored, Briddy."

"He ain't all that colored, Twig. He's got a bunch of white in him from his daddy's side of the family. He could pass as white if he wanted. Besides, it really shouldn't matter, should it? I don't think I'd care if he was black as a chunk of coal, I'd still love him. And Mama ain't gonna keep me from him. She's kept me from everything else, but not him."

Briddy was not allowed to wear makeup or stock-
ings. Most of her clothes, other than school uniforms, were hand-me-downs from cousins in
Albany, New York. She had never been allowed to
shop for clothes at Berry's, where all the girls her
age found the latest fashions. She was not allowed
to talk to boys on the telephone or go on dates.

Mrs. Roebuck had named Briddy after Saint
Brigid of Ireland. Brigid herded sheep when
she was a little girl. She eventually grew into
a beautiful young woman. Many noblemen
wanted to marry Brigid, but she chose to serve
God as a nun instead.

"Nun, my ass," Briddy often grumbled to herself.

Twig laid the scissors on the bed. He put his
hands in his lap. "Well, I think that's a little
better. At least it's all one length."

Briddy ran her hand across the top of her head.
"I hate our mother."

"Don't say that."

"Why not? She's a bitch. When's the last time she did something nice for you? Wash your sheets? Remember the time she spread them out on the front-yard bushes to embarrass you? Do you think maybe she'd take you to the doctor instead? See what's really wrong? Hell, no. It's all about her, Twig. It's all about God getting payback from poor, pitiful Henrietta Roebuck."

"I think we should pray to Saint Monica," Twig said.

"Jesus, another one of your saints. What's her story?"

"She's the patron saint of parents with wayward children."

"What the hell does that mean? You think I'm wayward? Shit, I'm normal. It's our mother who's all fucked up."

"Well, then, how about Saint Joseph? He helps with relationship troubles."

"Relationship troubles? Between who? Mama and the rest of the world?"

"No, you and Terrence."

"We don't have any trouble. I told you, we love each other."

"Yeah, you do. You got plenty of trouble. Mama ain't gonna let you see him no more. You heard what she said."

"Yeah, I heard her, but guess what?"

"What?"

"Terrence goes to *school* with me. He's in the symphonic band with me. And some of my classes, too. What's Mama gonna do? Take me out of the band? Take me out of Saint Tim's and put me in a public school with all the heathens? Shit, that'd be the day."

"Well, maybe you could at least not seem so 'around' him, if you know what I mean."

"No, I don't know what you mean."

"Well, like the article in the paper. The one that got your hair chopped off."

"Did you see my name in that story?" Briddy asked.

Twig was silent.

"Well, did you?"

"No, but it might as well have been there. It talked about your hair, and ain't nobody in the world got hair like yours."

"What hair?" Briddy laughed.

"You know what I mean."

The article appeared in the *Columbia Mail*, the city's afternoon newspaper. A reporter had covered Terrence's first day at Saint Timothy's:

While Columbia City Schools remained segregated when classes began today, a local parochial school opened its doors to its first Negro
student. Terrence Roberts, the 17-year-old
son of Sylvia and Matthew Roberts, arrived
at St. Timothy's Catholic School this morning. His entry into a previously all-white
parochial school was initiated by the recent
passage of a Roman Catholic diocesan pol-
icy that states that children will attend the
school in their territorial parish. It recog-
nizes that Negro Catholics are members of
personal parishes (i.e., parishes established
for the specific purpose of serving the Negro
Catholic community, generally founded
within the territorial boundaries of a white
Catholic parish) and notes that children of
those parishes have a choice to attend either
their personal (Negro) parish school or the
school of the territorial (white) parish.

Terrence and his father, Mr. Roberts,
arrived at St. Tim's shortly before the morning bell rang. They walked underneath an

arch whereupon the phrase "Enter to Learn, Learn to Serve" is chiseled.

Mr. Roberts shook his son's hand good-bye and Terrence was escorted by St. Tim's principal Father Thomas McClatchey to the school auditorium where approximately 150 other students were already seated in preparation for opening chapel and first-day orientation.

Terrence was dressed in the school uniform—black trousers and a white dress shirt with a purple school tie. Terrence chose to sit alone in the auditorium. Other students talked excitedly with friends and some watched Terrence carefully. Terrence looked about him but generally kept his head down, his eyes appearing to study his brown shoes. Several minutes later, a white female student with long, red hair entered the auditorium. She smiled when she saw Terrence and took a seat next to him. He smiled back at the girl and then seemed more relaxed.

Columbia City public schools also opened today. Despite the 1954 United States Supreme Court Brown vs. Board of Education decision that separate schools are not equal, city schools in Columbia remain segregated. However, the city's Negro leaders predict that a "selected" number of Negro students will be attending previously all-white high schools in the area by next fall.

"Well," Twig said, "I'm really sorry about your hair. It was beautiful."

"Thanks, buddy, but you know what?"

"Huh?"

"It'll grow back. Mama can't stop my hair from growing back any more than she can stop me from seeing Terrence."

Twig stared at a cabinet full of Briddy's band trophies. Briddy sat up.

"Hey," she said, putting a hand on his slim shoulder. "Enough about me. How are you doing? Doesn't seem like Mama's been hollering as much about wet sheets. Hollering about everything else, but not that."

Twig smiled. "Nope, she ain't been."

"How come? Are you still wetting the bed?"

"Not nearly as much."

"What's the secret?"

Twig's eyes grew big. "It *is* a secret."

What are you talking about?"

"I can't tell nobody. It's between me and Naomi."

"You and Naomi?"

"Yep, she's pretty cool."

Briddy stood up from the bed. She stretched her arms to the ceiling.

"OK, well, let me know if you do need some help."

"I will," Twig said, smiling again, "but I won't."

"Won't what?"

"Need any help."

"Well," Briddy said, studying herself in a mirror above her bureau, "I sure might. With this hair, I mean. Is there a saint that helps hair grow back fast?"

"Not that I know of, but there is Saint Expedite. He rushes prayers to God. He could rush a prayer about your hair."

"Do you really believe in all that crap?"

"Gotta believe in something."

"You know what, little brother?"

"Huh?"

"You're right. And you know what I believe in?
Even as fucked up as our family is?"

"What?"

"Love."

"What about that other thing?"

"What other thing?"

"I don't know, irresis-something."

"Yep, that, too. Irresistible desire."

CHAPTER NINE

Annie sat cross-legged on her mother and father's bed while Naomi fixed her hair. She studied the purple leaflet:

OLD-TIME HOLY GHOST HEALING REVIVAL!

UNDER THE BIG WHITE TENT

ACROSS FROM THE STATE FAIRGROUNDS ON ROSEWOOD DRIVE!

FEATURING BROTHER JEREMIAH J. WASHINGTON,

THE HOLY CHOIR OF HEAVENLY VOICES,

AND GOD'S MIRACLE GIRL!

SEE SIGNS AND WONDERS!

EXPERIENCE HEALINGS, PRAYER AND MUCH MORE!

"I want to go," Annie pleaded.

"Uh-uh," Naomi murmured, her mouth clasping several bobby pins. She smoothed her hair and pulled it into a tight curl at the nape of her neck.

"But I want to see the Miracle Girl! Please?"

Naomi pushed the last pin into place. "No."

"Why not?"

Naomi turned from Mrs. Mackey's vanity mirror. "First of all, I told your father you would be at Buck's. Second of all, the revival's for colored folks."

"It doesn't say that on here." Annie waved the leaflet in the air.

"It doesn't need to say it. Lots of things don't 'say' it. Now, aren't you going with Buck and Twig to the Old Lady for a little while?"

"Yeah."

"Well, just make sure you leave the farm before dark. I don't want you out there in the pitch black. I'll pick you up at Buck's when I get home. Mind your manners and make sure to thank Mrs. McCain for dinner."

"How long will you be gone?"

"A couple of hours, but no more. Now shoo. And be careful."

Buck, Twig, and Annie ran across First Field. The air was turning cool. They climbed into the Old Lady, glad for Friday to have finally arrived.

"How's Dead-Breath Devereaux?" Buck asked. He was hanging by his knees from a branch above Twig.

"Gross," Annie said, stretching out on her favorite thick branch.

169

Mrs. Devereaux taught seventh grade geometry at Crayton Junior High School. She had coffee breath and a habit of leaning in close to talk to students at their desks. Surviving her class was a rite of passage and how long you could hold your own breath.

"How's Briddy?" Annie asked Twig.

She'd only seen Briddy once since her hair had been shorn.

"She's OK. She said everybody talked about her hair after it first happened, but now nobody cares."

"What about Terrence?" Buck asked.

"Briddy said he said she looked even more beautiful than before. Said it was a sign they should be together."

"Hey, y'all!" Annie said. "Speaking of signs. You know that tent revival Naomi's going to out at the fairgrounds tonight? Well, I saw the leaflet about it. They're gonna have a Miracle Girl there. Signs and wonders too."

"We oughta go!" Buck said.

"But we're supposed to eat supper at your house," Annie responded.

"How would we get there?" Twig asked. "The fairgrounds are on the other side of town."

"Easy," Buck said, swinging back up to a sitting position. "The bus. One of 'em that stops at the shopping center goes all the way to the fairgrounds. It says on the front of the bus."

"What about being at your house for supper?" Annie persisted.

"We'll just tell Mom we're having pizza at Twig's house. She won't care."

"I don't know. What if Naomi sees us? She'll kill me. She already told me it was for colored people."

"Why's she gotta know we're there?"

"Well, I don't know."

"Com'on, y'all, let's go," Buck said, jumping down from the Old Lady.

"I'm in," Twig said. "I could use a miracle."

"Y'all sure Naomi won't see us?" Annie asked. "And we can't stay long. I have to be at Buck's house by the time she comes home."

"No sweat," Buck said, "let's go."

Annie, Buck, and Twig rode their bikes to Forest Lake Shopping Center and stashed them behind the grocery store. Bus No. 17 was pulling up to the curb in front of Rogers Pharmacy. It rolled to a stop and the folding doors slapped open.

"Fairgrounds?" the lean bus driver asked Buck.

"Yes, sir," he said, hopping on. Annie and Twig followed, slipping their dimes into the money machine. Annie liked the sound of the coins trickling down into the bottom of the tube.

The bus was warm and steamy inside. There was a row of seats open just behind the bus driver; Annie, Buck, and Twig stuffed into it. Twig pushed himself forward on the seat, making more room for Annie and Buck. He settled his elbows on the back of the bus driver's seat.

"Gonna get you a miracle, son?" the man asked Twig. He smelled like cigarette smoke and Aqua Velva aftershave.

"I just might, mister."

"Well, 'round all these niggers you're gonna need one. Heh, heh."

Annie jerked at Twig's shirt and motioned for him to sit back. Twig made a face and slid back into the seat.

The white revival tent stood out against the empty landscape of the state fairgrounds. The fair wouldn't arrive until October. Buck, Annie, and Twig led the way off the bus.

The tent was packed with people waving funeral home fans that read BOGART'S HOME FOR FUNERALS. PRECIOUS CARE FOR YOUR PRECIOUS ONES. Annie, Twig, and Buck found two empty seats at the back of the tent, behind a pole. They made Twig sit in the middle, on the split between the two folding chairs.

"Wonder where Naomi and Lily are?" Annie asked, searching the crowd.

"No telling," Buck answered.

Organ music began. Members of the Holy Choir of Heavenly Voices, dressed in gold robes, filed in and took their places on the stage. The music got louder and the choir began to sway back and forth. Suddenly, a beefy man in flowing purple robes appeared from a trapdoor in the middle of the stage. He wore a gold ring with a purple stone in its middle. He threw his arms into the air.

"*Praise the Lord!*" he bellowed.

Buck punched Twig. "Here we go!"

Twig moved forward on his seat so he could see. The man was now staring at the audience before him.

"Praise the Lord, brothers and sisters! My name is Brother Jeremiah J. Washington! Praise the Lord!"

The crowd began to move back and forth, much like the choir. Twig was transfixed. This was not at all like the stern, chilly process of a Catholic service.

"Brothers and sisters, let us begin tonight's services with a prayer. A special prayer for anyone who would like to come up to the stage and submit their request to me. But first, let us take up a love offering in the name of the Lord!"

Men in shiny, maroon suits appeared in the aisles and began passing silvery collection plates through the crowd. By the time a plate reached Annie, Buck, and Twig, it was over-flowing with money. The plates returned to the men in the aisles who delivered them to Brother Washington.

"Brothers and sisters, it appears that you have reached into your hearts and your pockets and found enough love for us to begin this service! Now, as I said, we would like to begin this special evening of prayer, praise, and miracles with a special request from a member of the audi-ence. Does anyone have a need to share with Brother Washington? A need to send skyward to the Lord by way of Brother Washington?"

Twig jumped to his feet like he'd sat on a hot plate. He scrambled down the row, excusing himself for stepping on folks' feet. He reached the aisle and ran to the front of the stage, where he took the steps up two at a time. Annie and Buck looked at each other.

"Holy shit," Buck murmured.

A large woman sitting next to Buck slapped the top of his head with a fan.

"Hey!" Buck groused.

"Shut your mouth," the woman barked.

Buck shut it, looking toward the stage. Annie watched too—carefully, scrunched down in her seat. Naomi was bound to see Twig and begin searching the crowd for her.

"Now what would be this young man's special prayer request today?"

Brother Washington pushed a microphone in front of Twig's face. Twig looked miniscule next to the titanic man. Twig stood with his feet set wide apart. The wider his feet spread apart, Annie knew, the more nervous he was. She prayed he wouldn't wet his pants.

Twig pulled on Brother Washington's sleeve and the preacher leaned down. Twig whispered in his ear. The audience was quiet, leaning forward toward the stage and the curious pair.

The choir swayed back and forth, humming softly. Brother Washington listened intently to Twig and then raised himself up.

"Brothers and sisters, my young friend, Nicholas, has a special prayer request that is of the upmost private nature."

"It's not *up*-most," Annie said to Buck. "It's *ut*-most."

The large woman sitting beside Buck glared at Annie.

"Sorry," Annie whispered.

Brother Washington motioned Twig to the floor. Twig lay stock still, his arms pinned against his sides and his eyes slammed shut. The preacher stomped the floor next to Twig and a resounding *whap* rang out. Annie jumped in her seat. Buck was sure the power of the man's foot had propelled Twig's small body a few inches off the floor.

"Lord Jesus, we ask you tonight to be with this young man and his prayer request. His heart is in the right place. His love for you is strong and true."

Brother Washington then knelt beside Twig and pressed his right hand on the boy's chest; his left hand rose into the air.

"Brothers and sisters, let us pray together for our friend Nicholas. May his request be granted. May his prayer find the Lord's listening ears. And may we all raise our hands to the heavens and say, 'Praise Jesus, amen!'"

A sea of dark hands rose to the tent ceiling. Two pairs of small white hands reached for the top of the tent too. "Praise Jesus, amen!" Brother Washington then spoke to Twig. Twig jumped up, a smile stretching across his face. He shook Brother Washington's hand and ran for the steps of the stage. When he reached the last step, Naomi appeared in front of him. She looked furious.

"Uh-oh," Annie said to Buck, "we better get out of here."

"What about Twig?"

"Well, let's at least get out of the tent."

Buck and Annie scrambled into the aisle and made it to the outside of the tent. Twig was not far behind. Nor was Naomi.

"What in the world are you children doing here?" Naomi said, her voice hard and fast.

"We were just curious," Buck said, backing into a thick rope tied to a large stake in the ground.

"Curious? Curious about what?"

"I don't know, a tent revival, I guess."

Naomi stepped forward and got close to Buck's face.

"You *guess*?"

"Please, Naomi," Annie piped up, "we didn't mean no—any—harm. We'll go home, right now. Com'on, Twig. Com'on, Buck. Let's get out of here."

"You just wait one minute, miss," Naomi said, grabbing Annie's collar. "How are you planning to get home?"

"Same way we got here," Twig sputtered. "The bus."

"Jesus," Naomi swore underneath her breath. "A bus full of colored folks?"

"Wasn't so bad," Twig said. "Everybody was nice 'cept the bus driver. And he was white."

"I see," Naomi said.

Lily rushed up behind them.

"What're they doing here?" she asked, excited.

"Nothing," Naomi said, angrily crossing her arms across her chest, "except going home. They have no business here."

"I had business here," Twig said, stepping up in front of Naomi.

"What kind of business?"

"Business."

"Well, the only business we're going to take care of now is getting you three home. I guess I'll have to go too."

"Here comes the bus now," Lily said.

"Will you be okay by yourself?" Naomi asked her friend.

"I'll be fine," Lily responded.

No. 17 pulled over to the side of the road not far from the tent. The door opened. Twig, Buck, Annie, and Naomi stepped aboard. The bus pulled away from the curb. The windows were foggy. Annie and Twig sat together. Naomi took a seat by herself. So did Buck.

Annie drew a picture on the window with her finger.

"What's that?" Twig asked.

"I don't know. A face, I reckon. So, what'd you ask Brother Washington to help you pray for? Whatever it was, must've been mighty important."

"It was," Twig said solemnly. "At least I think so."

"Well what was it?"

"For a period. I mean, I don't know exactly what a period is, but Briddy seems to be pretty upset 'cause she ain't got one. She's been in the bathroom a whole lot, crying about it."

Annie suddenly felt hot all over. Hotter than even the inside of the muggy bus made her feel. She wiped the face off the window. Maybe, just like Annie, Briddy was hoping to have her first period. But why in the world would she be crying about it?

"Twig?"

"Yeah?"

"I know this is gonna sound stupid, but when you're in the bathroom, do you ever see big wads of rolled-up toilet paper in the trash basket?" Annie saw these in the bathroom trashcan about once a month at her own house; her mother had explained to her what they were.

"Look like baseballs?" Twig asked.

"Yeah, you could say that."

"Yeah, I've seen those."

"Seen any lately? Like this month?"

"Nope, come to think of it."

The bus rolled through the foggy night. Past the beer joints on Rosewood Drive, through

the fancy old homes in the Heathwood neighborhood, and then out along Trenholm Road
toward the shopping center.

Annie stared out the bus window. All she
could think of were baseballs and how much
trouble she was going to be in with Naomi
when she got home. Naomi was sitting several rows behind her, staring out the window,
too. Annie was not sure, but she thought she
saw a tear running down Naomi's cheek.
Annie sunk as far into her bus seat as she
could.

"Naomi?" Annie whispered, knocking gently
on her parents' bedroom door. Naomi had
gone straight to bed, not saying a word to
Annie.

"Yes?"

"I'm, well, I'm sorry about tonight. We didn't
mean to make you mad. We just wanted to see
the revival."

"Why?" Naomi still did not invite Annie in the room.

"Well," Annie said through the door, "the Miracle Girl and all. And we never saw any kind of revival in a big tent like that."

"Well, now you have."

"Can I come in?"

"No, you can go to bed."

Annie touched the doorknob and then pulled her hand away. She went to her room and got into her bed. Her stomach felt terrible, and she began to cry. Naomi was mad, but now she was mad too. And she didn't know why.

"Annie?" It was Naomi, standing by Annie's bed.

"Go away," Annie said, her head turned away from Naomi. "I went away when you asked me to."

"I came to tell you I'm sorry."

"For what? It was a revival for colored people, not white people. We didn't have any business there. Just like you said."

"Well, I suppose I'm sorry you didn't have any business there."

Annie turned over and looked at Naomi. "I don't get it."

"I don't think I do either, but let's not go to bed angry with each other. Some sugar?"

Annie reached up and wrapped her arms around Naomi.

"I love you," Annie murmured.

"I love you, too."

If only it were that simple, Naomi thought, tucking Annie in.

CHAPTER TEN

O ctober came and with it the state fair, a wondrous two-week event that woke the south end of Columbia from an easy slumber into a cacophony of people, carnival rides, fried food, and farm animals.

Before he left for Charleston, Mr. Mackey had pressed $25 into Annie's hand. "Promise to ride the rollercoaster twice for me," he said, giving her a kiss.

"But Dad, you *hate* rollercoasters."

"I know, but your mama loves them and she always said riding it once was just a warm-up."

Mrs. McCain dropped Annie, Buck, and Twig off at the front gate of the fair, across from a squalid yard that had been turned into a parking lot. A tow-headed boy in overalls perched on top of a barrel under a tree; he held a homemade sign that read PARK—$1 DOLLER.

"Meet me right here at nine o'clock," Mrs. McCain said, "and don't be late."

"Aw, Mom, how 'bout ten?" Buck pleaded.

A horn blared behind Mrs. McCain's station wagon.

"Nine-thirty and no arguing. Now go."

Annie, Buck, and Twig tumbled out of the car like puppies out of a pen. They paid for their tickets, funneled through the gate, and joined a sweaty sea of people from all parts of the state and all walks of life.

"So," Twig hollered, "where y'all wanna meet if we get lost from each other?"

As much as she loved the little guy, Annie was hoping Twig *would* get lost from them, at least this one time.

"The Rocket, where else?" Buck said.

The Rocket was a disarmed Jupiter missile called *Columbia*. It rose sixty feet into the sky just inside the fairgrounds entrance. A bleached-blonde woman in a nearby booth was responsible for making lost and found announcements from the Rocket. She sucked on a cigarette, pushed a pencil and piece of paper through the greasy threshold of the booth, and asked for names.

"Write 'em down," she'd say, rounding one side of her mouth into an efficient O and aiming a stream of exhaled smoke at the threshold. Her announcements were drenched in thick, Southern syrup. "Jim-bo Wee-yums, meet yer mu-ther at the Raw-ket. Bi-yul Jon-sun, meet Lez-lie at the Raw-ket."

"So what d'y'all wanna do first?" Twig shouted above the din.

Annie knew what she wanted to do.

First, she wanted the sun to set, the sky to darken, and the air to cool. Then she wanted the rides to light the night with their bright, colorful bulbs. And then she wanted to get stuck with Buck in the most romantic place the state fair had to offer—a chair magically stopped at the top of the Ferris wheel. The chair would swing gently back and forth while riders on the ground were being loaded up. The lights and sounds of the fair would spread out underneath them. The smells of cotton candy, Fiske fries, and greasy sausage grinders would wend their way into the atmosphere.

And Buck would finally kiss her. Plain and simple.

The leathery-skinned man hustling folks onto the Ferris wheel looked at Buck before slamming the long chair-bar shut.

"Pretty little girl you got there, son," he grumbled, a cigar dangling from one side of his mouth. "Make sure you give 'er a kiss at the top. Good luck, you know."

Annie's heart lifted; the gnarly man winked at her.

Twig was across the way. Armed with a popgun that shot a cork the size of a marshmallow, he was aiming for plastic ducks as they floated by in a river of blue, food-colored water. Huge stuffed animals hung from the top of the game booth; Twig found the chance of winning one impossible to resist and had turned seventy-five cents over to a pock-faced carnie for five shots at the plastic waterfowl.

The Ferris wheel chair jerked and began its ascent. Annie grasped the bar, one hand close to Buck's. She hoped he would hold it, but he did not. When the chair stopped at the top, Buck kept busy surveying the sights below and pointing out rides they should try next.

By the time Mrs. McCain dropped Annie off at her house three hours later, Annie was batting back humiliated tears. She jumped out of the car and murmured, "Thank you." She tried not to slam the car door, made sure she slammed the house door, and once inside, ran to her bedroom where she slung that door shut too.

"Is something the matter?" Naomi asked, standing at the bedroom doorway.

"No," Annie said, throwing a tennis shoe on the floor.

"May I come in?"

"Suit yourself."

Naomi sat at the foot of Annie's bed.

"How was the fair?"

"How do you think?"

"Judging from all those slamming doors, I think not good. What happened?"

"I don't know. It's Buck. He's so weird."

"Well, it's late. Go brush your teeth and wash your face. Then we'll talk about it. A good girl talk."

Annie returned from the bathroom and got back in bed. She pulled the covers up to her chin and let out a long, exasperated breath.

"He had every chance to kiss me when we were on the Ferris wheel. It stopped at the top and it was just the two of us. Twig was playing that stupid duck game. Nobody could see us. It was perfect. The man running the ride even told Buck when we were getting on that it was good luck to kiss a girl at the top. But Buck wouldn't even hold my hand. He just stared off into space, talking about different rides he wanted to go on."

"Maybe he felt uncomfortable."

"Well, he sure doesn't feel uncomfortable sitting beside me in the cafeteria at school. The other day he made a girl move over so he could sit next to me. And he sure didn't feel uncomfortable telling me not to go getting a boyfriend at school. I just don't get it, Naomi. It's like he likes me but then he doesn't. Or he wants it a secret and he doesn't want to show it. That's not fair, is it? I know I'm the only stupid girl in the seventh grade who doesn't have an Aigner pocketbook, and I'm pretty sure I'm the only one who hasn't been kissed."

"Well, as for the first thing, your birthday's coming up soon, and as for the second thing, I doubt it."

Annie pulled the covers over her head. "I hate Buck."

Naomi pulled the covers back down. "Now, I doubt that too. Did I ever tell you what my Grandee used to say about men?"

"What?"

"She'd say, 'Mensies can be mighty funny sometimes.' "

"Mensies?"

"Men."

"I don't get it."

"Men are taught from the day they are born to be tough, to not show emotion, to not reveal themselves to others. I suspect Buck has been taught those things. He does not want to reveal himself to you, the way he feels about you. Have you ever seen him cry?"

"No."

"Has he ever seen you cry?"

"Sometimes."

"Why do you think that is?"

"Because I'm a girl?"

"More because he's a boy and he's been taught not to show his emotions. He has been taught, like most men, to hide his most inside self. I suspect you don't know half as much as you think you do about Buck."

"Really? Like what?"

"Like what stirs around inside him when he's trying to go to sleep at night. Like the feelings running around inside him when he's with you."

"What kind of feelings?"

"Good ones, scary ones, surprising ones. All kinds of feelings that make a boy wonder what's going on with himself. And you know what?"

"What?"

"One day he'll sort those feelings out."

"Then what?"

"Who knows? Maybe you'll get that kiss you're looking for. But in the meantime, you know something else Grandee used to say about men?"

"What?"

"Well, it's not very nice, but it's kind of funny…"

"What?"

"Well, sometimes she'd say a man was like a fart in a mitten."

"A fart in a mitten?"

"Yes, meaning they bump around inside themselves and have a hard time getting out. Meaning, I think, they have a hard time figuring out who they are and what they really want."

Halloween arrived on a warm, sultry night two weeks later. Annie, Twig, and Buck stood out on the street. They were at their first stop—the Wilsons, where, if they were lucky, Mrs. Wilson would be giving away homemade caramel-covered popcorn balls wrapped in wax paper.

"There they are," Buck whispered. "See Mrs. Wilson? She's knitting those baby booties again."

Buck's eyes were fixed on the wide picture window that illuminated the Wilsons' living room. Dr. Wilson and his wife, Lillian, spent almost every evening there. A black-and-white television flickered in one corner of the room. Dr. Wilson read by the light of a tall lamp set to one side of an easy chair; his wife sat on a sofa, knitting. Buck was convinced that Mrs. Wilson was knitting baby booties for the babies she never had.

The Wilsons were childless and took care of their prize-winning camellia bushes the way other folks tended to children. A string of blue ribbons ran the length of the Wilsons' garden shed. Every year, the couple entered their best blossoms in the Columbia Garden Show.

"How do you know she's knitting baby booties?" Twig whispered.

"You ain't got to whisper," Buck said. "They can't hear us out here."

"Well, maybe she's knitting something else."

"Maybe," Buck said, "but I doubt it. So, y'all ready to get our popcorn balls?"

Annie was reluctant about going to the Wilsons since she had run over one of their camellias with her bike. She hadn't meant to, but she had swerved off the road to avoid a squirrel that had no idea which way it wanted to go.

"I reckon," Annie said.

Just as the three began to make their way down the Wilsons' sidewalk, a souped-up

Malibu spun around the corner and screeched to a stop in front of them.

"Well, lookie here," said Jack, Buck's big brother. His large head appeared from the driver side window. Several boys were in the car with him.

"What y'all doing?" Jack asked in a singsongy voice. "Trick or treating?"

"Leave us alone, Jack," Buck stammered. Ugly, sitting beside Buck, whimpered.

"Well, fellas," Jack boasted, turning to his buddies in the car, "just listen to the big man talk. He wants us to leave 'em alone."

Jack returned his attention to Buck. Then he looked at Annie.

"Buck ever kiss you?"

Annie wanted to run. She hated Jack. And she knew Buck hated him too.

Buck pushed Annie away and stepped forward. "Shut up."

Jack jumped from the car. "What'd you say?"

Buck held his ground; his fists were clenched. "Shut up."

The boys in the Malibu snickered. Jack— a tall, stringy teen—towered over Buck.

"You know what, little brother? You kiss Annie on the lips and I'll shut up. Prove to me you got a real pecker in those pants. Prove you ain't no queer. 'Cause that's exactly what you are. A fuckin' fairy. I read that shit you wrote in your..."

Buck plowed headfirst into Jack's midsection. Jack fell backward against the car, gasping for air. Annie and Twig stood stock-still. Buck looked at both of them and then took off through the dark night. Ugly raced after him.

Jack got his breath back. "Where'd that little piece of shit go?"

"I don't know," Twig mumbled.

"You don't know? You queer too?"

Twig was silent; Jack popped him on the head. "Talk to me, midget. You Buck's little boyfriend? Y'all play Hide the Salami?"

"No," Twig stammered. Warm piss spilled into his pants. He placed his hands in front of him to cover the wet.

"What a fuckin' twerp," Jack growled, climbing back into the car. "Sure you aren't Buck's little boyfriend?"

Jack then turned on Annie. " 'Cause I sure as hell know you ain't Buck's girlfriend."

"Yes, I am. He's not a queer. He's just..."

"He's just what? Has he ever tried to get a little feel? Ever stuck his tongue in your mouth? Never mind, don't even bothering saying nothing. I know the answer."

With that, Jack shot the bird at Twig and Annie. The car squealed away, leaving a smell of burned rubber and a trail of blue smoke.

Twig and Annie stood out on the street. The Wilsons' front door opened.

"Get down," Twig cried, grabbing Annie's arm.

Twig and Annie crouched on the asphalt, hoping Dr. Wilson wouldn't see them. In the quiet, they could hear Mrs. Wilson call from the living room, asking her husband if everything was all right. He stood in the yellow glow of the porch light, looking around the front yard.

"I don't see anything," he called out, closing the front door.

Twig looked at Annie. "Wanna go to the Old Lady?"

"What about your pants? They're wet."

"Don't matter. Let's go."

Twig and Annie walked through the dark. When they reached the barbed wire fence, Annie wadded up the brown grocery bag she'd brought along for collecting candy. She threw it in the woods.

First Field was awash in moonshine. The Old Lady stood quietly in the distance, her silhouette black and solid against the indigo skyline.

"Jack is such a jerk," Annie grumbled, following Twig along the path.

"I know."

"Buck's not a queer."

"I know that too."

"Wonder what Jack was talking about. You know, about what Buck wrote."

"Search me. Maybe he keeps a diary."

"Boys don't do that."

"How do you know?"

"I guess I don't. So what's going on with Briddy?"

"Mama's raising all kinds of you-know-what about Terrence over at school. She wants Terrence kicked out. The nuns have been told not to let them be anywhere together, and they're not in any of the same classes anymore. Briddy says it's all a bunch of bullshit. She's reading some weird kind of book right now. It's called *The Feminine Mystique*. It's all about women having equal rights and stuff."

"Like colored people?"

"I guess sorta so."

Annie and Twig reached the Old Lady. They climbed into her branches and settled in their spots.

Annie rested her head against the bark of the tree. "Did I tell you I'm going to see my mom for Thanksgiving? Daddy and I are going to fly to Maryland."

"That's cool. I'll make sure I pray to Saint Raphael."

"What does he do?"

"Takes care of travelers. Have you ever been on a plane before?"

"Nope. Naomi says I'm gonna be journey proud."

"What does that mean?"

"Means you get so excited about going on a trip that you can't sleep the night before. Something like that. Anyway, hey, Twig?"

"Yeah?"

"I been thinking a lot about Briddy. I gotta ask you something."

"Shoot."

"Remember when you were praying for her to have a period…"

"I know what a period is now."

"Well, has she had one? 'Cause if she hasn't…"

"What?"

"Well, it's kind of complicated, but if she's been having her period and now she's not and she and Terrence have been—well, you know—then, well, she might be pregnant. You know, having a baby."

"I know what pregnant means, and I know she ain't having a baby. She'd be big as the side of a barn if she was, and she ain't."

"But babies don't start out real big. Sometimes you can't tell for a long time."

"Well, I could tell. Just like you can tell Buck ain't no fairy."

An owl hooted from the direction of the old barn. It was a lonely call. A breeze picked up and ruffled through the Old Lady's branches. The air had cooled. Annie wrapped her arms around her knees.

"Hey Twig, what would you do if someone tried to hurt the Old Lady? You know, cut her down or something."

"I'd climb in her and not come out. They'd have to cut me down too."

"You remember that time we came over here and Mr. Montague was here with those men? We'd never met him and we thought all those men were going to chop her down."

"Yeah, I remember."

It had been several summers ago. Halfway across First Field, Twig was the first to see the men gathered under the live oak. Two of them held chain saws in their hands; another, a ladder.

"Hey!" Twig hollered, throwing his stick on the ground and breaking into a run. "What're y'all doing?"

The men turned and looked. Twig reached the place where they stood, planting his feet firmly in the earth underneath the Old Lady. A tall, older man stepped forward. He wore faded jeans, a yellow cotton shirt, and a felt cowboy hat the color of a fawn. His face was deeply tanned and kind.

"I don't believe we've had the pleasure of meeting," he said.

"Name's Twig Roebuck. I'm a friend of this tree. Her name's the Old Lady. Y'all aren't planning to chop her down or nothing, are ya? 'Cause if you are, we got a problem."

"And my name's Manning Montague. It's nice to meet you, Mr. Roebuck."

The two shook hands.

"Pleased to meet you, sir, but you can just call me Twig. And this is Buck and Annie behind me. We live in Shimmering Pines, but we come over here a lot to sit in the Old Lady."

"The who?"

"The Old Lady. That's what we call her. One time Annie's dad told us she was real old, older than all of us put together, if you know what I mean. And she's real beautiful, too. Mr. Mackey didn't tell us that. We could see it for ourselves."

Mr. Montague took his hat off and wiped his brow. He looked into the live oak's thick canopy. "She is quite beautiful, isn't she?"

"Yes, sir, she sure is, and we love her."

"Well, I do too, son, but one of her largest branches is sick, and we need to tend to it before it makes the rest of her sick. We may have to take the limb off. That one up there. Can you see it?"

Mr. Montague pointed to a branch that was not the same umber hue as the rest of the limbs.

"Yes, sir, I see it. Been wondering why it was a different color."

"Because it's diseased."

"But how'd you know it was sick? I mean, you live in North Carolina, right?"

"Yes, I live with my sister now, in Saluda. We look after each other in our old age. But this tree and I have been friends for so long that even now, not being here, I know when she's not feeling well."

Mr. Montague leaned close to Twig and whispered. "Some folks would think I'm crazy saying this, but she lets me know. Kind of talks to me, if you know what I mean, and I think you may."

A grin spread across Twig's face. "Yes, sir! I know exactly what you mean. The Old Lady talks to us too."

"Well, I'll tell you what then. If you and your buddies will let us get to work, I suspect the Old Lady will be feeling better by this afternoon and you can come back then. I don't want anybody in the way when we take that branch down."

"Will it hurt?" Twig asked.

"Don't think so."

"Uh, Mr. Montague?"

"Yes, son?"

"You ain't never gonna let nothing happen to the Old Lady, are you?"

"Not as long as I can help it. What about you and your friends?"

"No, sir. We ain't either. We love her."

"Well, then," Mr. Montague said, "it sounds like she's in good hands."

The wind played softly in the Old Lady. Annie studied her hands in the moonlight. She hoped they were as good as Mr. Montague said they were.

Twig inspected his pants. They were beginning to dry. "Annie?"

"Yeah?"

"You know, Naomi helped me quit peeing in my bed. I don't know why I peed in my pants tonight. I reckon Jack just scared the daylights out of me. He's awful mean, ain't he?"

"He sure is."

"Well, at least I don't wet my bed no more."

"How'd you do it? I mean, how'd you quit pee-ing in your bed?"

"Grew my bladder."

"Grew your bladder?"

"Yep, I drank more water and held my pee longer every day and my bladder got bigger. Sorta like filling a balloon with water. A little bit at a time, though. I can hold my whiz all night now. Me and Naomi kept a schedule with how much water to drink and when to go. It was kind of cool. A chart with a lot of numbers and times. Naomi said I was so good at keeping numbers that I ought to be a businessman when I grow up. I ain't never thought about that. I reckon I just always thought about being a saint, you know?"

"But isn't being a saint kind of a hard thing to do? Don't you have to perform miracles and stuff like that? Then don't you have to prove it to a whole bunch of people?"

"Something like that, but come to think of it, I've already done my miracle. I ain't wetting my bed no more. So maybe I better think about being a businessman."

"Maybe."

CHAPTER ELEVEN

Rose Hill Hospital and Sanitorium was a secluded place, nestled on the banks of the Chesapeake Bay in northeastern Maryland.

Annie wore her best Sunday outfit—a gray jumper and jacket—to see her mother. Mr. Mackey held Annie's hand as they climbed the steps of a venerable brick mansion, the visitors' center where they were to meet Mrs. Mackey.

"Nervous?" her father asked.

"A little. I wonder how she looks?"

"I bet she'll look happy to see you."

"What should I say?"

"Whatever you want, but give her a big hug first, OK?"

"OK."

Mr. Mackey and Annie pushed through the heavy front door and were greeted by a soft-spoken woman who ushered them into a comfortable sitting room.

"Your mother has been looking so forward to seeing you," she said to Annie, smiling.

"Who are you?"

"I'm sorry, I should have introduced myself. I'm your mother's doctor. Jane Neuman. I've heard so much about you that perhaps I felt we'd already been introduced."

"You've heard a lot about me?"

"Yes, your mother misses you so much and she enjoys nothing more than to talk about you and all that you do."

"Really? I thought all she cared about was my brother."

Dr. Neuman and Mr. Mackey glanced at one another. Dr. Neuman leaned forward and grasped Annie's hand.

"She cares about you just as much, and that is one thing she wants to tell you when you see her."

"When will that be?"

"Why, right now, I believe."

Mrs. Mackey stood in the doorway. Her hair was pulled back from her face. She wore a simple pink sweater over a white shirt and a beige skirt.

"Annie?"

"Mom!" Annie ran to her mother and burrowed into her slim waistline.

Mrs. Mackey kneeled on the floor in front of Annie and put her hands on her daughter's shoulders. "Let me look at you."

Annie stepped back.

"My God, you are so beautiful. And you're growing up."

"Really?"

Mrs. Mackey pulled Annie back to her chest and began to cry—deep, wracking sobs. Annie pushed away from her mother.

"Mama? What's wrong? Why are you crying? I thought you would be happy to see me."

Dr. Neuman put a hand on Annie's shoulder. "She is, but why don't we give your mother a chance to compose herself?"

"What does that mean?"

"Calm down a little. Your mother *is* happy to see you, but she..."

"She what? She's so happy to see me she's crying?"

"Annie!" Mr. Mackey's voice was stern.

"I knew this is how it would be!" Annie cried. "I just knew it. Mama still misses Will, and it doesn't matter that I am here. None of it matters except my brother and he's dead."

Annie flew from the room and out the front door. She tripped on the last step, regained her balance, and ran until she found a mossy brick path that led to a secluded garden surrounded by dense boxwoods. Inside the garden were several benches. Annie liked the secretive spot. She sat down and inspected her right shoe. A deep scratch sliced across the toe of the glossy, black patent leather. The shoes were new, and they were a step up from traditional Mary Janes. They had half-inch heels and straps that swiveled over the top of the foot or rotated to rest against the back of the shoe.

Annie rubbed the scratch.

"Some scratches won't go away, will they?" Dr. Neuman appeared at the garden entrance.

"I can fix it," Annie murmured, rubbing harder.

"May I sit down?"

"Sure."

Dr. Neuman eased onto the bench beside Annie. "What if you can't fix it?"

"Well, I guess I'll have a shoe with a scratch on it. Or Daddy will take 'em to Gerald's in Five Points. That's a shoe shop in Columbia. The whole place smells like shoe polish. It won't be like having a new pair of shoes anymore, but it'll be OK."

"Having a new pair of shoes is a wonderful feeling, isn't it?"

"Yes, ma'am."

"I remember as a little girl, at the beginning of the summer, going to get a new pair of tennis shoes. They would be so pretty and white, and I loved the way they smelled. So perfect! But then I would wear them and they would get dirty. It was the same with new saddle shoes every fall. I suppose it's just hard to keep anything new and perfect, isn't it?"

Annie looked at the doctor quizzically. "Are you trying to tell me something? This sounds like one of those adult talks where you're talking about one thing but you really mean something else."

Dr. Neuman smiled. "Your mother told me you were very smart, and she is very right. I do mean something else."

"What, then?"

"Your mother is a little like your shoes. She's very pretty, but she's been scratched and she's not new anymore. And when I say 'new', I mean that she is not whole anymore. She is not as much of the mother you used to know. She is not the same mother you had before your brother died. She is different now."

"How different?"

"Well, let's see. More emotional, more fragile, more careful as she goes about her life in this world."

Annie sighed. "That doesn't sound so good. I thought she was getting fixed up here."

"*Mended* might be a better word. But even if you take your shoe to the shoe shop, it will never be quite the same, will it? Your mother will not be the same as she was before your brother died, and that's what you need to know."

"So everything's changed?"

"Some things, not everything."

"What hasn't changed?"

"How much she loves you."

Annie rolled her eyes. "But you saw her bawling in there. Why did I make her cry? Why wasn't she happy to see me?"

"She *was* happy to see you, it just came out in a different way than you are used to. I believe a lot of her tears in there were about being relieved."

"Relieved?"

"Relieved that she still has you. Relieved that she still has your father. Relieved that she feels like she can come home one day soon and be your mother and your father's wife again."

"But is she going to explode like that every time she sees me from now on?"

"No, I don't think so, but I do think she wants you to come back to the big house as soon as

you can. She has a surprise for you. Your birthday is soon, am I right?"

"December first."

"Well, in that case, I think we should get
moving."

Annie followed Dr. Neuman back to the mansion.
Once inside, she directed Annie to a smaller
room down the hallway. The door was closed.

"Go ahead, knock," Dr. Neuman advised.

Annie knocked softly.

"Maybe a little harder?"

Annie knocked again.

"Come in!" Annie's mother exclaimed.

Annie opened the door. Her mother and
father stood at a round table just inside the
pretty room. A chocolate cake, with fourteen

candles—including one to grow on—sat in the middle of the table. Presents surrounded it.

"Happy birthday!" her mother and father shouted.

Annie smiled. "Is this all for me?"

"All for you!" her mother said, embracing her daughter.

On Friday morning, November 22, the silver Piedmont DC-3 rolled down the runway and pulled into the chilly, crystalline sky over Baltimore. It banked hard to the left and roared south toward Columbia.

"Thanksgiving was fun," Annie told her father, seated beside her, "and I love my birthday presents."

"I'm glad you do. You know, your mom and Dr. Neuman went to Baltimore and picked all those things out. I think they did a good job, don't you?"

"I sure do." Annie couldn't wait to get home and go to school wearing her new clothes—several Villager shirts and skirts, a Villager dress, an Aigner fish-basket pocketbook, and a gold circle pin. She also got two pairs of new shoes—a pair of red Pappagallos and a pair of brown Weejuns. Plus, Bonnie Doon socks and a London Fog raincoat. And if that wasn't enough to be over the moon about, Annie's mother gave her a pouch of Maybelline makeup and a set of hot rollers.

"It's time you take those braids out and show off that beautiful hair of yours," Mrs. Mackey had said to Annie. "But not too much makeup, promise?"

"Promise."

Mrs. Mackey hugged her daughter hard. "I will see you before Christmas, OK?"

"Why can't you come home now? With us?"

"I have a little more work to do with Dr. Neuman."

"But you promise? In time for Christmas?"

"I promise. In time for Christmas."

The DC-3's propellers plowed through the November air. The flight to Columbia was several hours long. Annie's father had settled into his aisle seat with a copy of the *Baltimore Sun*. Annie, in a window seat, stared out at the clouds. She thought they didn't look a thing like the cotton puffs she'd pasted on blue construction paper when she was in elementary school.

It was early afternoon, about 1:30 p.m., when the pilot's voice came over the intercom. "Ladies and gentleman, Captain Williams here. I'm sorry to interrupt whatever you may be doing, but I have some disturbing news that has been radioed to me from the Baltimore tower."

Annie looked at her father, about to speak. He put his finger to his lips.

"ABC Radio News has issued a special bulletin from Dallas, Texas. Three shots have been fired at President Kennedy's motorcade. As you probably know, the president and the first lady are on a three-day trip to Texas. The president's motorcade was making its way from Love Field to downtown Dallas when the shots were fired. As more details are radioed to us, I will share them with you."

Annie's father looked stunned.

"Did anybody get hurt?" Annie asked.

"I hope not. For this country's sake, I hope not."

The DC-3 continued its path toward Columbia. Some passengers talked quietly with one another; others simply listened to the groan of the airplane's engines.

An hour later, Captain Williams's voice came over the intercom again. It sounded shaky. "Ladies and gentlemen, I...well, I have some terrible news. CBS News is reporting that President Kennedy has been assassinated. Our president is dead, ladies and gentlemen. He was taken to Parkland Hospital where doctors were unable to revive him. If—Jesus, this is difficult—if there is a pastor on board with us today, I would ask that he come forward and lead us in a prayer for our country, the Kennedy family, and our safe passage to Columbia."

Annie looked at her father. Tears rolled down his face.

"Daddy?"

"Shh, baby. Here, get in my lap. Let me hold you."

Annie crawled into her father's lap. As she did, a large, dark man walked forward from the back of the airplane. His right hand held a black Bible stuffed with snippets of paper. On his index finger was a gold ring with a purple stone in its middle.

"Daddy, that's the preacher! That's Mr. Washington from the tent revival."

Mr. Mackey held his daughter tighter. "Shh, baby. We need be quiet now."

Brother Washington disappeared into the pilots' cabin; several minutes later his voice rolled out into the airplane's interior like a rumble of thunder.

"Brothers and sisters, my name is Brother Jeremiah J. Washington. In this time of upmost need for our country and for the Kennedy family, I am honored and humbled to be called into service. God is a mighty king; rest assured he has us in his great and loving hands as we traverse these clear skies and this troubled day. I would like to begin by reciting the twenty-third Psalm. Join me if you wish. *The Lord is my shepherd, I shall not want. He makes me lie down in green pastures; he leads me beside still waters…*"

Annie closed her eyes and listened to her father follow along with Brother Washington's words. She didn't say anything about the preacher using the word *upmost*. Something told her it didn't matter now. And maybe it never did. Instead, she thought of Naomi, who loved President Kennedy. Then she thought of her mother and scratches and things that could never be mended.

"I'm sick of everybody watching TV," Buck said from his branch in the Old Lady, "but I reckon it's better than having to go to church. I mean, it's terrible about President Kennedy and all, but it's sure nice not having to go to Sunday school and all that stuff."

"Daddy said it's history in the making and that we should try to watch as much of it as we can," Annie said.

She was picking at a hole in the knee of her jeans. It was a cold Sunday morning. The wide trunk of the Old Lady shielded Annie against a chilly breeze.

"Well, I, for one, ain't watching any more of it," Twig said. "We got enough crying going on at my house as it is."

"What's going on?" Annie asked.

"Terrence is gone."

"Where to?"

"Back to New Jersey. Just before Thanksgiving. You must've been in Maryland when he left.

"She was," Buck confirmed.

"How come he left?" Annie asked.

"Whole family left. I reckon 'cause Mama was raising so much hell. Somebody said stuff was painted all over their house too."

"What kind of stuff?" Annie asked.

"KKK," Buck said. "Shit like that."

"Briddy'll hardly come out of her room now," Twig said. "She quit the band and stuck her clarinet under the back tire of Mama's car. Mama ran over it backing out of the garage. Terrence called the house once, and Mama answered the phone. She screamed at him never to call again. I don't think he will. Anyway, what about your mom? When's she coming home?"

"Before Christmas," Annie answered.

"How's she doing?" Buck asked.

"She's better, but not perfect."

"Nobody's perfect," Twig said.

Annie looked toward First Field. "Is that Briddy?"

Briddy was wrapped in a loose-fitting sweatshirt. She held her arms around herself, marching along the deer path with a mission she was clearly not happy about.

"Geez," Buck said from high in the tree, "she looks pissed."

"She *stays* pissed," Twig said.

Briddy arrived at the base of the Old Lady, pointing at Twig. "Mama says you've gotta come home right now."

"How come?"

"Lee Harvey Oswald—the man who killed the president—well, he just got shot and killed too. He was walking through the jail when a man stepped out and shot him. The whole thing happened right on TV. Mama watched it and started screaming. She says the world's coming to an end and we're all going to church to pray. So let's go."

"Shit," Twig muttered, scrambling down the tree.

He reached the bottom, grabbed his stick, and turned to Buck and Annie. "Y'all say your prayers to Saint Genevieve."

"What does she do?" Annie asked.

"Helps out in disasters. Especially real big ones."

CHAPTER TWELVE

Mrs. Mackey touched Annie's shoulder. "Sweetie, wake up, you may want to look outside. It's snowing. Hard."

Annie opened her eyes. Her mother was sitting on her bed, holding a cup of coffee.

"Are you kidding me?" It was late March, an odd time for any kind of snow in Columbia, much less a big snow.

"No, I'm not. See for yourself. School's cancelled."

Annie jumped from underneath her warm covers and peered out the window. She caught her breath. Shimmering Pines was a winter wonderland. Sweet, white snow was everywhere. On the trees, on the grass, on the driveways, on the mailboxes. Annie had never seen so much snow in her life. A foot of it had fallen during the night, and big, fat flakes were still pouring out of the gray, heavy sky.

Annie jumped out of bed, hugged her mother, and ran for the kitchen telephone. She didn't know who to call first. Buck? Twig? Maybe, Annie thought, even Briddy would be unable to resist the temptation of such a big, unexpected snowfall. Maybe she would come out from her self-imposed exile since Terrence had left last November.

"Before you go out, I want you to eat something," Mrs. Mackey said. She'd returned to the kitchen with Annie and was reading the morning newspaper which brandished a big headline on the front page: LET IT SNOW!

"Is Naomi coming today?"

"I've already called her and told her to stay put. I doubt the buses are running anyway."

"Where's Dad?"

"In the carport trying to get his car started. He's determined to get to work."

Annie reached into a kitchen cabinet for some cereal. She didn't want to waste time waiting for her mother to cook something. Wasted time meant melted snow.

"Before you go out, look in your brother's closet. I put some heavy winter clothes in there. Some gloves and hats and that sort of thing. There might even be a pair of Will's boots in there. They'll be too big for you, but with enough socks, I think they'll keep your feet warm, OK?"

"OK," Annie said, finishing her cereal.

One change in Annie's mother since she had come home from Maryland was her ability to talk about Will. With Naomi's help, Mrs. Mackey had also been able to go into Will's room and gather up most of his clothes for the thrift store. The door to the room was left open now, and while it still contained vestiges of Will's things—his baseball trophies, his books, a baseball cap—it also had new accoutrements that made the room less of a shrine and more of a place for good memories.

"Mom," Annie said.

"Hmm?"

"I love you."

"I love you too," Mrs. Mackey said, peering over her reading glasses. "Now listen, are y'all going to the farm?"

"Yes, ma'am."

"Well, be careful out there."

"We will."

"And stay off that pond. I can't stand to think of that poor little Ugly falling through, much less one of you."

"We will."

"Promise?" Mrs. Mackey grabbed Annie's wrist and squeezed it hard. Her voice was urgent, pleading. "I mean, really, promise? I can't have something…"

Mrs. Mackey still had moments of sudden alarm, almost panic, and Annie knew to respect these times. She grasped her mother's hands and looked into her eyes. "I know, Mom. I promise."

Mrs. Mackey smiled weakly. "Well, while you're getting dressed, I'll make some hot chocolate. You can take it with you in a thermos. It will help keep you all warm."

"Thanks, Mom."

Annie called Twig and Buck and they agreed to meet at the fence. Twig said Briddy was coming later, when she woke up. Twig also said he was bringing a real sled. The Roebucks, originally from Minnesota, had all kinds of interesting foul-weather equipment stored in their garage—a Flexible Flyer sled, a pair of ice skates that hung off a nail, and a wide snow shovel that stood in a corner.

Buck brought along a cookie sheet for sliding, and so did Annie.

The farm shone like polished alabaster. First Field was a stunning sight. Annie almost hated to make tracks in the silky smoothness of it all.

The Old Lady stood on the bluff, a white behemoth. Buck, Annie, and Twig stopped there and Annie stashed the big, silver thermos in a crook of the Old Lady's trunk. She put the Styrofoam cups her mama had sent her with there too. Then the threesome ran for the edge of the bluff where the sledding was bound to be good.

The bluff fell off at a gentle grade into the bottom fields. The ride on a sled or cookie sheet was long and fast, well worth the time and effort it took to climb back up the hill in the dense snow.

Annie, Buck, and Twig rested at the top of the bluff after several rides down. The snow had not slowed up and the sky was still dark. Pregnant with possibilities.

"Ain't it just beautiful?" Twig said, sitting on his sled and drinking a steaming cup of hot chocolate.

"Sure is," Buck replied.

Later in the morning, Annie, Buck, and Twig walked back home across First Field. They were wet and cold and needed to change into dry clothes, but they promised to get together again in the afternoon. Maybe, they hoped, Briddy would join them by then.

The afternoon sky had lightened up, and the snow had stopped falling. Except for the children's voices, the farm was quiet, insulated from sound by the heavy snow that blanketed the fields and woods like a down comforter.

Briddy tramped across First Field and joined Annie, Buck, and Twig. Her hair had grown back since last year and it bounced out from underneath her knit cap. She declined to sled down the hill and set about building a snowman instead. The snow was perfect for it, she explained. Briddy worked hard to push the balls of snow into place. Buck helped her while Annie and Twig continued to sled.

Buck was looking for anything that would make a good nose for the snowman when Briddy bent over and gripped her midsection.

"What's wrong?" Buck asked.

"Nothing," Briddy replied.

Briddy was putting her knit hat on the snow-man's head when she cried out. She fell to her knees and doubled over in the snow.

"Good grief, Briddy!" Buck cried. "What's wrong?"

"I'm—um—oh, shit, I think I'm having a baby."

"*You're what?*" Buck stepped back in the snow, stunned.

"You heard me. I'm having a baby. Either that or it's bad cramps. Real bad. But I don't think so. I think it's a baby. But it's way too early."

Briddy sank deeper into the snow. Her eyes closed and she reached for Buck. "Help me," she whispered. "It's too soon."

Buck turned toward the bluff and screamed for Twig and Annie. They were at the bottom of the hill, making angels in the snow.

"What was that?" Twig asked Annie.

Buck screamed again, louder.

"Sounds like Buck!" Annie replied. "Sounds like something's wrong!"

Annie and Twig abandoned the sled and a cookie sheet and ran hard up the hill. At the top, they could see Buck waving for them. Briddy was lying in the snow, curled up. Annie thought of her mother, curled up in Will's bed. Whatever was going on, her gut told her it was bound to be bad.

"Hurry, y'all!" Buck hollered. "Briddy's having a baby!"

"*A what?*" Annie screamed, gasping for air as she ran through the thick snow.

"You heard me," Buck cried, "a baby."

Twig reached Briddy and Buck first. He fell to his knees in the snow. He clasped his hands in prayer.

"Goddernit, Twig, get up!" Buck screamed. He grabbed Twig's jacket and yanked him out of the snow. "We gotta help Briddy!"

Briddy grabbed Buck's arm, "I can't go home."

Buck, Twig, and Annie looked at one another.

"Well, then, where?" Twig whispered.

"Underneath the Old Lady. Please, underneath the Old Lady. She'll take care of me. Won't she, Twig? Won't she take care of me?"

Twig was silent.

"No," Buck said. "We need to go to the barn. There's horse blankets and shelter there. It will be warmer. Here, Annie, you get on one side of Briddy. I'll get on the other. Twig, go ahead of us and start getting the blankets. There's a bunch of 'em stacked up near the feed bins. Get as many as you can and put 'em on the floor. We gotta keep Briddy warm."

"We gotta go home," Twig stammered. "Briddy can't have no baby in that barn."

Briddy grabbed Twig's jacket. "Yes, I can!" she cried. "I'll have the baby right there. Then we'll let it die. That was my plan. It's horrible, but I was gonna have it and let it die when the time came. But it's two months early now. It'll probably be dead anyway. We'll bury it. Right here on the farm. Under the Old Lady. Nobody but us will ever have to know anything. Us and the Old Lady."

Twig's eyes grew huge. His lower lip trembled. "We can't do that. We just can't let a baby die."

"Why can't we?" Briddy said, her teeth clenched. "What else am I gonna do? Have a baby? A *colored* baby?"

Briddy's eyes closed again. She began to groan. A low, painful sound. Annie could not speak. She felt light and far away.

"Annie," Buck hollered, "you have to help me get Briddy to the barn. Twig, go get the damn blankets. And get a shovel too. There's one in a stall. I've seen it before."

"I ain't doing it," Twig said. "I just can't."

"Goddernit, Twig," Buck screamed, "you *have* to! You heard Briddy. She's right. She can't have no baby, and she sure can't have no half colored baby. There ain't no place in the world for such as that. Now *go!* Get the blankets and the shovel."

Twig turned and ran for the barn. Annie and Buck lifted Briddy to her feet.

"Com'on now, you gotta help us a little," Buck said to Briddy. "Try to get your feet underneath you."

"How in the world are we going to do this?" Annie cried.

"We're gonna do it, period. Mama's always talking about how babies are born. Briddy's labor pains are real bad and coming real fast.

If this baby ain't s'posed to come for another two months, then it's bound to be tiny and premature. That's good. For Briddy, at least. It'll come out easy. Now com'on, Annie, we gotta get her to the barn."

Briddy lay on several blankets, with several more covering her. Still, she shivered. Her face was white. Sweat dampened the hair around her temples. Twig kneeled by her side, praying. This time, to Saint Ulric, protector of mothers against birth complications.

"Dear Saint Ulric, please take care of Briddy and..."

"*And go get the damn shovel!*" Buck screamed.

Twig scrambled up off his knees, crossed himself, and ran for the stall. Annie knelt on the other side of Briddy, holding her hand. Another labor pain came and Annie thought Briddy would break her hand, she was gripping it so tightly. Buck lifted the blankets away from Briddy's legs.

"OK, Briddy. I gotta get your pants off."

Briddy murmured something.

"Now," Buck said, "bend your knees."

"Ohh..." Briddy moaned.

"Just keep 'em bent, Briddy," Buck instructed. "This ain't gonna take long. I can see the baby's head. It's a tiny little thing, but it's coming. It sure is. Now *push!*"

Briddy leaned forward from her waist. Her face was bright red; the veins on the side of her neck had grown huge.

Twig appeared with the shovel. "Is it here yet?"

"Almost," Annie whispered.

Briddy cried out one more time.

"Holy Jesus!" Buck cried. "It's a baby! It's a dadgum little baby boy!"

PART TWO

CHAPTER THIRTEEN

It was still early. Not even 9:00 a.m. Annie made a list of things she needed to do. She loved lists, especially when she was able to cross off items with a fat, black slash of her Sharpie pen.

Call Tom and Delores.

Call Dorsey (feed Lucy, get mail and newspapers).

Tent, food, clothes, toiletries.

Letter to the editor.

Cleaning out the coffee pot, Annie decided her mission could be nothing less than saving the Old Lady from destruction. She could not save the entire farm, but one tree? One lovely old tree? And thus what was buried beneath it? Surely she could do this. She *had* to do at least this.

The dark coffee swirled around the sink and down the drain. Suddenly Annie felt warm all over. A hot flash? Or the resident angst of her middle-aged life? Never mind being a successful artist, creating sculptures out of trash, out of things that other folks dispensed with as junk. It had not been enough to make her feel worthy.

It should have been, a $200-an-hour therapist once tried to convince her, and it could be, he counseled, if only she would "tread more lightly" upon herself, if only she would reflect more often upon her accomplishments as opposed to her self-imposed failures. The marriage. The miscarriage and her unconscionable relief. The inability to save her mother from the bleak cavern of depression that she repeatedly visited and eventually never returned from. Her sweet, dear father, slowly dying of a disease that left him addled, suspicious, and often unable to identify anything—including his daughter.

Annie grasped the side of the sink. "Breathe," she told herself. "Just breathe."

Annie's mother died two years ago. Her heart had been failing. Other vital organs followed suit. A host of well-intentioned doctors had plied their trade upon Mrs. Mackey's frail, bruised body. Eventually, a wise, matronly nurse took Annie aside and told her recovery was not to be. "Your mother is dying," she'd said. "You should make the doctors quit the tests. She is suffering terribly. You should insist they make your mother comfortable now. It's time."

The morphine had settled her mother like a baby being rocked to sleep. Hours before her death, Annie held her hand. It was thin, reed-like.

"Mama," Annie whispered, "can you hear me?"

Mrs. Mackey nodded ever so slightly. Her mouth puckered as if to say something, but she did not.

"Mama, are you ready to go?" Annie had read somewhere that dying people often waited for "permission" to let go of life.

"I don't know," Mrs. Mackey murmured. "Maybe."

"It's OK if you want to. Delores and I will take care of Daddy."

"Mmm."

"Mama," Annie persevered, "you were a good mother to me."

Mrs. Mackey's eyes fluttered open. She shook her head ever so slightly back and forth. "I tried," she whispered.

Annie had driven home late that night; the doctors had said her mother would likely live for another day or so. A sitter relieved Annie, who needed the rest she could not get in the hospital room, curled into a too-small sofa, waiting for the next intrusion of nurses, technicians, dieticians, even the infernally chipper woman who came by to take a survey of her mother's hospital stay.

Annie's cell phone had rung just as she was crossing the Blossom Street Bridge.

"Mrs. Hart?"

"Yes?"

"This is Nurse Williams on the fourth floor at Providence. We need you to return to the hospital."

"What? Why? Is my mother OK?"

"Ma'am, I'm sorry, but all I am allowed to tell you is that you should return to the hospital."

Annie's heart thudded in her chest; the lights of oncoming cars blurred together. She tried to focus.

"Have you called my father?"

"No, ma'am, your instructions were to only call you."

"Right. Thank you, I'm on my way."

The hospital room was dark, save for a dim light in the corner of the room, over the sink. Annie's mother was in the bed, covered carefully in a fresh, white blanket. Her head, turned to one side, lay on a pillow. Her eyes were closed and her hair was combed, but her mouth was contorted, as if she had cried out, not wanting to be alone, not wanting to die.

Her mother's solitary death was another thing Annie could not forgive herself for, and after twelve sessions with the therapist, she and he agreed that they were getting nowhere. The erudite man had held his fingertips together and peered at her from behind owlish, horn-rimmed glasses. His assessment of the situation rang as true as a horseshoe around a stake.

"Despite the troubled relationship with your mother, the circumstances of her death, and the other things we have discussed, I believe there's still something you're not willing to share with me, something that is troubling you very much. Am I right?"

Annie did not answer.

"Annie," he said, leaning forward, "until you are able to discuss whatever that is with me, I am wasting your time and your money."

"And right now you're wasting even more time," Annie scolded herself, reaching for the sprayer to send the last of the coffee grounds down the disposal.

In the den, she sat at her mother's graceful mahogany desk. Annie was always amazed to find that when she opened its long center drawer, she was met by the faint smell of her mother's Charlie perfume. It was comforting.

Annie put her hand on the phone—the old-fashioned kind, tethered to the wall. She was not sure what she would say to Tom. That she may need his help? That she was planning to pitch a tent in front of the Old Lady, protest its destruction, and plead for its preservation? Tom could make a will as tight as the paper on the wall, but what did he know of someone trying to save a live oak tree? And would he even want to help her if he could? He did love the outdoors, she knew. So maybe, just maybe.

Then there was the call to Delores, the affable woman who looked after her father at his cottage at Caroliniana Retirement Community. She would need to know that Annie wouldn't be coming to visit her father for several days. Delores would not press for details, but Annie would ask Delores to tell her father that she was going to be out of town. That is, if he wondered where she was. Or who she was. Sometimes her father remembered her, sometimes he didn't.

Talking to Dorsey would be the easiest call to make. He was Annie's best friend, an interior designer who outfitted homes with a subtle elegance sought after throughout the Southeast. Dorsey would be delighted by Annie's intentions; he wouldn't shy away from helping her in any way he could, including feeding her sinister, six-toed Hemingway cat, Lucy.

Annie dialed Dorsey's cell phone; he answered promptly. "Hello, beautiful! Will you marry me?"

Annie smiled. "I'll have to think about it."

Always, Dorsey asked Annie to marry him. It was a standing joke that had a hint of real possibility to it. No complications, like middle-aged sex. Just plain good company with a gay man who cooked like crazy, kept an immaculate house, and understood her like no other person in the world.

"Dorsey?"

"Yes, my dear?"

"I need to ask a favor of you. Well, several actually."

"Anything. You know that."

"Well, I'm getting ready to save a tree. It's that live oak tree I've always told you about. The one we used to climb in when we were kids. The one on the farm next to Shimmering Pines, where I grew up. We called her the Old Lady. There's a story in today's paper about the farm. They're getting ready to develop it."

"The Montague property?"

"One and the same."

"I read about that, but why would they tear down the tree?"

"Because she's on the bluff where they're planning to build the condos. There's only one bluff out there, and the Old Lady is smack-dab in the middle of it. Developers don't like working around things, like trees. They'll chop her down as quick as they can get their chain saws cranked."

"Are you going to be like one of those tree-sitters in California? Saving the redwoods?"

"Well, I hope I can just pitch a tent and hang out underneath the Old Lady, but if I have to tree-sit, I will. I just haven't worked out all the details."

"You know what I say about details."

"Don't let the details get in the way of the endeavor."

"Precisely. So what can I do for you?"

Annie let out a deep breath; maybe her plan wasn't so outlandish after all.

"Well, for starters, you can help me get set up under the Old Lady. I need to go there tonight, after midnight. I'm going to take one of Tom's old tents and some of his camping gear. Can we take the Antichrist?"

The Antichrist was Dorsey's beat-up, blue Suburban, circa 1977. Dorsey loved to wend his way up the winding driveways of fashionable homes in Atlanta's Buckhead community behind the wheel of the wheezing, old-school automobile.

"And I need you to feed Lucy while I'm gone."

"Only if I can use a slingshot."

"Oh, Dorse, she's not *that* bad."

"She's pretty damn bad, but I'll manage. Now, how long do you think all this will take?"

"I have no idea."

Dorsey promised to pick up Annie at her house at 11:00 p.m. Relieved to have taken the first step, she dialed Tom's office number.

"Hart, Ballenger, and Lines," a receptionist announced crisply. "May I help you?"

"Tom Hart, please."

"May I ask who's calling?"

"Annie Hart."

"One moment, please."

Annie waited on the line; she and Tom had not spoken to one another for several months.

"Long time," Tom answered. "How are you?"

"Fine. Well, not really."

"What's up?"

"I need your advice. Your legal advice."

"Shoot."

Tom never wasted words; there had been many times during their marriage when Annie wished he would. It softened the blow of tough conversations.

"OK, well, here goes. I want to save an old tree. A very old, magnificent live oak tree on the Montague property, near where I grew up."

"What do you mean, save it?"

"Did you read this morning's newspaper?"

"Briefly."

"There was a story about the Montague property, on the front page, in the bottom corner."

"It's been sold, right? They plan to develop it?"

"Yep."

"That's a shame, but, unfortunately, under-standable, given where it is."

"But what if I want to save the tree? It means a lot to me. I used to play in it all the time, with my friends in the old neighborhood. We called her the Old Lady. She's on the bluff, where the development is supposed to begin."

"I see. So, assuming they have plans to tear it down, how do you plan to save it?"

"Protect it. I mean, get in front of it, or climb into it. You know, guard it."

"Annie, it's a tree. You know how much I love nature. I'm sure it's an extraordinary speci-men, as most live oaks are. And I don't mean to ignore your sentimental attachment to it, but..."

"But what if there's more than just the tree I'm trying to protect?"

"Like what?"

"Like a burial site."

"Whoa, what are you talking about?"

"What if there's a baby buried..."

"Stop right there."

"Why?"

"I don't know where this conversation is leading, but I'm not a criminal defense attorney and..."

"Tom, I don't need a criminal defense attorney! No crime has been committed. I just want to save the Old Lady."

"Are you sure?"

"Sure I want to save the Old Lady? Yes. I've never been so sure about anything in my life."

"Annie, I'm asking if you're sure that no crime has been committed."

Annie hesitated.

"Tom, please just promise you'll help me if I need it."

"Jesus, Annie."

"Tom, I'm begging here."

"You know how to reach me."

"Thanks."

Annie breathed a sigh of relief and called Delores, who reported that Annie's father was eating his breakfast and watching CNN; he loved *Headline News*. Annie said she would not be able to see him for a few days but could be reached on her cell phone in case of an emergency.

Delores did not seem intrigued one way or the other. "Yes, ma'am."

Two strikes off her to-do list. Annie turned on her laptop.

Dear Editor,

I must take issue with a statement made by a spokesman for the Manning Montague family concerning the development of condominiums on the old Montague farm property. In an effort to rationalize the destruction of a natural sanctuary miraculously set next to the crowded and congested city limits of Columbia, the spokesman said he didn't know of anything on the undeveloped property other than 'a falling-down barn, some old corn fields, and plenty of kudzu.' I take strong issue with that statement.

This lovely old farm was once my second home, a short hike from the neighborhood where I grew up. The farm is an undisturbed world of wide fields, lovely trees and quiet ponds. It is home to hawks, deer, birds, and foxes. In particular, there is a magnificent Southern live oak tree set on a bluff where, as I understand it, the condominiums are to be located.

Though I would like to see the entire Montague property saved from disturbance and reserved as a natural preserve, I realize that is probably asking the impossible. However, I would like to see that the live oak tree and a small parcel of land around it are saved from destruction. To that end, I will do my level best to protect the tree until an agreement with developers can be reached for the tree's welfare. By the time this letter is published in your paper, I plan to be stationed at the tree and pursuing its protection.

Sincerely,

Annabelle Mackey Hart

Annie reread the letter and printed it out. She would deliver it to the newspaper's editorial office after lunch.

Dorsey arrived in the Antichrist promptly at 11:00 p.m.

"Ready?" he asked.

"Ready," Annie replied.

They packed up her supplies and pulled out of the driveway. Driving across town, Annie thought about whether to tell Dorsey about the baby. Maybe, she hoped, the Old Lady could be saved on her own merits. Maybe the matter of the baby would never have to surface. She remained quiet, staring out into the dimly lit streets of downtown Columbia as the Antichrist rolled along.

"Mighty quiet over there," Dorsey remarked.

"Just thinking."

Office buildings turned into city neighborhoods. Trenholm Road had been widened to a fat, four-lane thoroughfare and Forest Lake Shopping Center had been transformed into an upscale office and retail complex. The simple one-story and split-level homes of Shimmering Pines had disappeared. In their stead was a gated residential community called The Preserve, brandishing mammoth brick houses surrounded by elaborate landscaping.

Annie felt her heart quicken.

"Slow down," she cautioned, "we should be getting close."

Annie spotted a big CONGAREE DEVELOPMENT GROUP sign. It was posted in the ground at the front gate to the farm.

"This is it," Annie said.

Dorsey pulled the Antichrist off the road and dimmed the headlights. "Hurry," he said.

Annie hopped out and checked the gate; it was not locked, just secured with a long chain looped several times around a fence post. She grappled with the chain and swung the gate open. Dorsey drove the Suburban through. Annie pulled the gate shut.

"Whew," she whispered, jumping back into the 'Burb.

Dorsey commandeered the Antichrist down the narrow, dirt road leading into the heart of the Montague property. Annie took in the atmosphere around her. It was so dark, away from city lights, but she could see ghostly Spanish moss hanging in the trees that grew on either side of the road. A low-slung critter trundled across the road ahead of them. Its eyes turned toward the car and gleamed in the headlights.

"Possum," Annie said.

"Or coon. Either way, should've brought my stew pot."

"I really appreciate you doing this."

"Happy to. How're you feeling? Glad to be back?"

"Actually, pretty nervous. Lots to think about, lots of memories, too, you know?"

"Good ones, I hope?"

"Mostly."

Plink.

A pebble hit Annie's bedroom window in the wee hours of the morning after the late-afternoon birth of Briddy's baby.

"Annie!" she heard Twig calling. "Open your window!"

Annie crawled from her bed and pushed up the window. Cold air rushed in around her. Twig stood in the snow below. He was still wearing his father's work boots and the clothes he had on earlier in the day.

"What do *you* want?" she demanded.

"I want to tell you something." Twig's arms were wrapped around his midsection. He stamped his feet in the snow.

"What time is it?"

"It's late, well, early. Early in the morning. I came to tell you the baby *was* dead. It wasn't alive like I thought it was, like I said it was."

"How do you know?"

"I went back there, after we left the farm. Buck was still sitting in the barn with Briddy and the baby. It was dead, didn't make a noise. Buck was crying. He was holding the baby in his arms. Briddy was asleep. I made Buck give the baby to me, and I made him take Briddy home. When they left, I wrapped the baby up real good and buried it. Right where Briddy wanted. Underneath the Old Lady. I said some prayers too. Sorta like a funeral. Saint Nicholas and the Old Lady are taking care of that little feller now."

"Saint Nicholas? Nicholas is your name."

"I know, ain't that something? Mama named me after the saint who takes care of kids. Even ones that go straight to heaven, I reckon. Anyway, it's OK now. You gotta believe that,

Annie. It's OK. We done all we could. We really did."

Annie stared down at her friend; he was shivering.

"Are you sure, Twig? I mean *really* sure?"

"Positive. Now I gotta git."

Annie pushed the window closed and scrambled back into bed. Her eyes had just closed when she heard another *plink*. Twig had returned.

Annie pushed the window open again. "*What now?*"

"I forgot to tell you one more thing. I already told Buck and Briddy. We ain't never talking about the baby again. Not to each other, not to Naomi, and not to nobody else either. Just like Buck said, there ain't no baby. So, you swear?"

"Swear."

Twig turned in the dwindling night and headed for home. His work boots left a trail of slick, silvery impressions in the fallen snow.

Dorsey brought the Antichrist to a stop in front of the barn. One side of the structure had caved in. The other side leaned precipitously toward the ground. Several sheets of rusted tin had peeled away from the barn roof, curling like an old lady's hairdo.

"Where to from here?" Dorsey asked.

"Follow the road. When it ends, we should run into First Field and that should take us across to the bluff."

The road did not last long; the Antichrist lurched over First Field. Stiff, high grass scraped like sandpaper against the belly of the Suburban. Annie held her breath. Surely, she prayed, they were getting close to the bluff. She looked at Dorsey. His eyes were trained ahead, both hands grasped the steering wheel.

"Holy mother of God!" he exclaimed, slamming on the brakes.

Annie braced herself against the sudden stop; her eyes followed Dorsey's astonished gaze.

In the distance, the Old Lady loomed like a majestic spirit of unprecedented proportions. She was half real, half dream. Buttery and soothing, moonlight poured down through her branches, which stretched across the bluff like giant arms—arms that reached for Annie.

CHAPTER FOURTEEN

orsey stood back from the tent. Its garish blue nylon siding clung to supple poles.

"Well, there's not much I can do about the décor, but it appears to be stable. That's a good thing. So, you're sure you've got everything you need? I'm not crazy about leaving you out here by yourself."

"I'll be fine," Annie answered. "The Old Lady will look after me."

"I suppose she will. So you'll call me first thing in the morning?"

"Will do. And first thing in the morning, you'll call the newspaper and the television stations?"

"I'm on it."

"Thanks, Dorse. Don't know what I'd do without you."

"I'm glad to be a part of this. I never knew a tree could be so inspiring. If this thing takes off like I think it will, there's no telling what will happen."

"I don't want too much to happen. I just want to save the Old Lady."

"I know you do, and everybody who sees her and has got any sense will feel the same way. It's like the Angel Oak of Charleston. How this tree remained such a secret is beyond me."

"Mr. Montague was a private man. And I'm sure his descendants haven't wanted to spread the news of what's out here, other than choice spots for pricey condos—pricey condos for people who will hire *you* to decorate them. Talk about irony!"

"Won't touch the first one if the Old Lady isn't saved."

"Promise?"

"Cross my heart."

Dorsey cranked the Antichrist. It grumbled to a start and lumbered away from the bluff like an old bear. When Annie could no longer see brake lights in the distance, she turned to the live oak. Suddenly, she felt weary. "Well, I guess I'll say goodnight. Probably got a pretty big day ahead of us tomorrow."

A tendril of Spanish moss, hanging from a low branch, swayed ever so slightly in the night air.

Annie zipped the tent's opening closed. She stripped down to her underpants and a T-shirt and crawled into her sleeping bag. She heard an owl's plaintive hoot. The earth underneath her smelled rich and pungent. She wondered where, among the Old Lady's roots, Twig had laid the little boy to rest. He never said, but the notion of a tiny body, wrapped in Buck's Yankees sweatshirt, did not bother Annie as she thought it might have.

Rather, Annie decided, it encouraged her.

"Wherever you are," she whispered, "you will be safe."

The dawn chatter of birds high in the canopy of the Old Lady woke Annie from a deep sleep. She opened her eyes and reached for her watch, stashed in a small pocket hanging on the inside of the tent—7:00 a.m. She kicked out of the warm bag, put her clothes on, and pulled her hair into a hasty ponytail. When she unzipped the tent door, a chipmunk stared at her from his perch on an impressive root.

Annie smiled. "Looks like you've got yourself a good spot."

The chipmunk seemed oblivious to her presence.

Annie found a nearby bush, squatted, and peed. She ate a cereal bar and made her coffee by way of a battery-operated percolator. It came out a little strong, but it was good all the same.

She inspected the Old Lady's branches, easily finding her favorite limb from so long ago. Annie climbed into the tree and settled on the sway-backed branch. Below her, the chipmunk hunted for his breakfast. Annie finished her coffee, tossed the travel mug to the ground, and reached for her cell phone when an ominous rumble reverberated across the morning landscape.

Three yellow bulldozers rolled across First Field. Several trucks followed, lurching across the uneven terrain. Annie's hands grasped the branch. The bulldozers continued their forward march across the field. Annie had often wondered what it would be like to fight in a war, to wait for the enemy's charge. Now she knew.

She felt helpless, paralyzed in her spot in the Old Lady.

The bulldozers made a final assault upon the bluff and pulled to a stop. A white truck arrived, emblazoned with signs that said CONGAREE DEVELOPMENT GROUP. Two green trucks also pulled up, emblazoned with DEMPSEY TREE AND STUMP REMOVAL—DEMPSEY DOES IT RIGHT DOWN TO THE ROOT.

A well-dressed man emerged from the white truck. "What the hell is that?" he asked, pointing to the tent.

"Looks like a tent to me," said a burly man on top of a bulldozer.

Cautiously, the man walked around the tent. "Hello? Anyone home?"

Annie swallowed hard, said a prayer, and made her move.

"Up here. In the tree."

The man swung around; he was tall and slender.

"My name's Annie. Annie Hart."

"Uh, Bill Turner. Congaree Development. Now who'd you say you were?"

"Annabelle Hart. I'm here to save this tree."

"Say again?" Perplexed, Turner stepped closer to the Old Lady.

"Listen, Bill—may I call you Bill?"

"Help yourself."

"I don't mean to get off on the wrong foot with you, but I'm here to save this tree. I don't want y'all cutting it down. It needs protecting, and I'm here to do that."

Turner rested his hands on his hips. Annie plowed ahead. "Until we come to an agreement, I'm staying put."

Turner cocked his head. "Now let me see if I've got this right. You're trespassing on Congaree property, and you're planning to sit in this tree until we agree not to tear it down, even though it's my company's tree to do with whatever we want to? Is that it?"

"In a nutshell."

"We'll see about that," Turner grumbled. He turned to the men on the bulldozers, motioning them forward.

"Whoa, now, mister," said the burly one, "I ain't knocking down no dang tree with a lady in it. Especially a pretty one."

Annie smiled at the man; he tipped his ball cap. "Name's Joe, ma'am. Joe Dempsey. Top o' the morning to you!"

Turner turned on Dempsey. "You let me handle this."

"Why, yes, sir, just trying to make conversation." Dempsey smirked and winked at Annie.

"Well, quit trying. We hired you to clear this bluff, not chitchat."

Turner turned back to Annie. "Now let me ask you one more question before I call my boss and the authorities."

"Shoot."

"Is this some kind of prank? Today is my birthday, and this is precisely the kind of joke some of my buddies at work might come up with."

"Damn good one," Dempsey muttered.

"No," Annie replied, "it's not a joke. I don't want this tree destroyed. She's old and beautiful and deserves her peace."

"And you understand that if you do not get out of that tree, get your gear, and get out of here that I'm going to start making calls?"

"I do. And for what it's worth, happy birthday."

"Yeah, thanks," Turner snorted, flipping his cell phone open.

"Hey, boss," Dempsey announced cheerfully, "looks like we got company!"

A mobile television truck bumped across First Field, following the path blazed by the bulldozers.

"Shit!" Turner growled. "No one says a fucking word but me."

"Does that include the lady in the tree?" Dempsey asked. He winked at Annie again.

Turner eyed Dempsey. "Do you want this job?"

"I do, but time's a wastin'. We got other jobs we could be working on."

"I understand," Turner replied. "Give me an hour."

Before the hour was up, the area around the Old Lady had turned into a small circus. Two sheriff's deputies had arrived, blue lights flashing. Shortly thereafter, several more Congaree employees had appeared on the scene. The WIS-TV camera crew had set up on one side of the Old Lady, a reporter and a photographer with the *Record* on the other.

Dorsey arrived shortly thereafter.

"Good morning, dear!" he shouted, emerging from the Antichrist.

"Hey!" Annie shouted back.

"How'd you sleep?"

"Blissfully."

"Is there anything you need?"

"Call Tom. I don't have any cell phone service up here. And lunch."

"Will do."

A deputy stepped toward Dorsey. "Sir, may I ask who you are?"

"A friend of Mrs. Hart's. She's the lady in the tree."

"Yes, sir, I got that, but you'll need to leave the property immediately."

"And if I don't?"

"I'm afraid we'll have to arrest you for trespassing."

"Go to it!" Dorsey smiled and turned to the reporters. "Pens ready? Camera rolling?"

The deputy looked at the men in suits. "What d'ya want me to do?"

"Leave him alone," Turner snapped. "At least for the time being."

"Same for the press?" the deputy asked.

"Same for the press. Sheriff Babson is on his way, as well as our attorney."

The press contingent convened as close to Annie as possible.

"Ma'am, I'm Diane Wise with WIS-TV," said a reporter. "We'd like to talk you. Ask you a few questions."

"What do you want to know?"

"Well, for starters, your name. And what you're doing up in that tree."

"My name is Annabelle Hart. H-A-R-T. I'm here to save this live oak from destruction, but that's all I want to say until my attorney comes. Can you wait? It shouldn't be long."

"We'll wait," Ms. Wise answered.

"Thank you." Annie began a second prayer. This one, for a small miracle—that Tom would actually come.

Twenty minutes later, Tom, Sheriff Babson, and two Congaree attorneys gathered on the bluff. The sheriff had a red nose and a greasy forehead. Tom asked to speak to Annie privately.

"Make it snappy," the sheriff barked, hooking his thumbs in his fat cop belt.

Tom stepped over the yellow police tape and made his way under the umbrella of branches. He peered up at Annie. "Mind coming down here for a minute? Nobody else needs to hear our conversation."

"Not a chance. You come up."

Tom looked exasperated already. "You want me to climb up there?"

"I do. *Please.* If I come down, it's all over."

"Jesus," Tom swore underneath his breath. He tucked his tie into his shirt, rolled his sleeves up, and took his shoes off. Behind him, a camera clicked. Tom climbed into the Old Lady and maneuvered carefully across the thick branch to Annie's perch.

"I'm hardly dressed for the occasion," he groaned, lowering himself to a sitting position.

"You're fine. Thanks for coming."

"You may not want to thank me after I tell you that you need to get down out of this tree and off this property before you're arrested. I agree with you, it is a beautiful tree, but Babson and Congaree mean business. You're trespassing, interfering with business, and you're liable for money and time wasted."

"I thought an attorney listened to his client's side of the story before dispensing advice."

"I'm all ears."

Annie closed her eyes. The promise she'd made so long ago was about to be broken.

She felt the Old Lady sigh and whisper, "It's OK."

Annie opened her eyes; Tom was watching closely.

"There's a baby buried somewhere among the roots of this tree," she said. "I'm not exactly sure where, but somewhere."

"I'm sorry, I must not have heard correctly. Did you just say a baby? Buried here?"

"Yes, a baby."

Tom shifted his weight, took off his glasses, and rubbed his eyes.

"Tell me the story, but slowly. Very slowly. If I ask you to stop, I want you to stop. Got it?"

"Got it."

Annie relayed the details of the baby's birth. "No one did anything wrong, Tom. The baby was stillborn and buried underneath the roots of this tree somewhere. No one knows about it but the four of us. We kept it a secret."

"Holy shit."

"I agree. Holy shit. But you see now why I can't let them push the Old Lady over or disturb the ground around it. I mean, not only is this tree so worth saving, but this is a burial site, right?"

"Well, yes, Annie, it is, but it also sounds like it could be construed as the site of something far more serious, like a crime. You know, something akin to manslaughter. I mean, this isn't my line of legal work, as you know, but it might be argued that the baby could have survived if it had been taken to a hospital."

Annie shut her eyes and held her breath. Tom had just said the one thing she didn't want to hear. The argument she'd been having with herself most of her life. The searing possibility that the baby could have been saved. But no, Twig had stood in the snow at the bottom of her window and said otherwise.

Annie opened her eyes and looked at her ex-husband.

"Tom, we were *kids*. What was Briddy going to do? Tromp home through the snow after she'd just had a baby? Ask her bitch of a mother to take her to the hospital because she'd just delivered a child? Never mind a child with a black father."

"Are you absolutely *sure* the baby was stillborn?"

"Twig said it was."

"All right, I've got to make some calls."

Annie began to tremble. A tear rolled down her face, then another.

"Jesus, please don't cry, Annie."

SALLEY MCADEN MCINERNEY

"But you said manslaughter, Tom."

"I shouldn't have said that. I don't know what kind of charges would apply to a situation like this. If any would apply at all. But let's not worry about that right this minute. Let's just keep the bulldozers away from the tree. What do you say?"

"OK."

"Here's a handkerchief. Fresh."

"Thanks," Annie mumbled, blowing her nose.

"Now, listen. I need to tell the press something. I need to tell the cops something. And I need to talk with Congaree. Then there's the solicitor's office—no way they're not gonna get involved."

"The solicitor's office? But why?"

"Two reasons. Solicitor Barnes is a political animal. One of the worst. He's got a nose for

305

cases that help him keep a high profile among voters. If he sees a possibility of being in the limelight, he'll be all over this thing. Like white on rice, my daddy used to say. He may even be helpful. Who knows."

"Well, I'm not leaving the tree. No way."

"I understand that, but if it comes down to it, are you prepared for the story to come out? I can't see how we're going to avoid some kind of disclosure about the baby's body. In fact, I'm pretty sure it's illegal not to disclose such information. In the meantime, the press is going to go crazy over this story. And I don't just mean local yahoos. I'm talking Fox, CNN, and all that good stuff. Are you game?"

"Yes, I think I am, but what about the others? Twig, Buck, and Briddy?"

"I don't know. Where are they?"

"No clue."

"Well, good, let's keep it that way. For the moment, I'm simply going to tell the cops, Congaree, and the press that there is the possibility this tree holds a state record of size or some such bullshit as that—historical significance, whatever—and that it should be protected from destruction until we can sort things out. It's a leaky boat, but maybe the contention will give us some time above water. The argument won't last for long, but perhaps long enough for me to figure some things out, call some friends who know more about this kind of stuff. Otherwise..."

"There is no otherwise, Tom."

"Gee, thanks, Annie, but can you just hang with me here?"

"I can. But what about the press? What if they want to talk to me?"

"Keep your mouth shut. Let me do the talking for the time being, OK?"

"OK." Annie reached for Tom's hand and squeezed it.

Tom made his way back to earth. The *Record* reporter asked him how long Annie was planning to stay in the Old Lady.

Tom looked up at Annie and returned his gaze to the reporter. "As long as it takes to insure that this tree is protected from destruction."

CHAPTER FIFTEEN

Early in the evening, Annie devoured a Whopper Junior, fries, and a Coke. Afterwards, she stretched out on top of her sleeping bag, hands behind her head. The farm was tranquil, save for a pair of pin-striped mockingbirds making a stir.

After a long day, Annie was tired.

Tom had stood beneath the Old Lady with a Burger King bag in one hand and a soft drink in the other. It was late afternoon. His shirttail was out, his tie was gone. "No onions, right?"

"Right!" Annie reached down from her seat on a low branch. "Thanks so much. I'm famished."

"Figured you would be."

"Tom?"

"Yeah?"

"Would you call Delores, at Dad's place, and let her know I don't have cell phone service out here? I just want to make sure Daddy is OK."

"No problem. I'm pretty sure I still have the number. And Annie?"

"Yeah?"

"I'm really proud of you. You're absolutely right—this tree is a treasure. I hope we can save it on its natural merits, without having to wade into anything else."

"The baby?"

"Yeah, the baby. Jesus, I mean the more I think about it. You guys were *kids*. And one of those kids had a baby. And it died. And..."

"And it wasn't all *Ozzie and Harriet*, was it?"

"No, it wasn't. I just hope we don't have to tell the whole world about it."

"I hope we don't either."

"Well, we've got a ways to go, but I might have a rabbit up my sleeve."

"What kind of rabbit?"

"Henry Porter."

"The guy running for governor?"

"Yep. Big environmentalist, as you probably know. It just so happens his chief of staff and I were fraternity brothers at Clemson. I've got a call into him. Hope to hear back before too long."

"You think he would get involved in this?"

"It's a possibility. Publicity you can't pay for and an issue that's right up his alley. Why not? But we'll see."

With bad press looming like a tornado warning over the development project, Tom had struck a deal with the posse of tight-lipped Congaree attorneys—Annie would be allowed to stay put for twenty-four hours while the future of the Old Lady was "discussed."

And just as Tom predicted, Solicitor Barnes turned up in short order to sweeten the deal. Clearly delighted to be in front of cameras and reporters, the corpulent man with stringy hair raked across his sweaty head cited "an interesting case of civil disobedience and the possibility of a preservation issue." Barnes halted further construction activity until the matter was "settled satisfactorily."

Deputy Sheriff Beanie Harris was posted at the site of the Old Lady. Her polyester uniform did little to enhance her figure, which was shaped like a plump summer squash.

The press contingent, buzzing like a swarm of honeybees, was redirected to the entry of the farm, where several more deputies parked their gray and blue police cruisers in front of the gate and a crowd of curious onlookers and placard-waving preservationists gathered.

By lunchtime, WIS-TV's *Noonday News* had aired the first story of Annie and her quest to save the Old Lady from destruction. The story was picked up regionally, then nationally. A camera crew from CNN in Atlanta showed up by midafternoon. When the crew was told that it would not be allowed on the property, a helicopter was hired. Local TV stations and newspapers joined the winged campaign, turning the sky over the farm into an air show. By early evening, the story of Annie and the Old Lady had spread like a Texas brush fire—it was the talk of the town, the airwaves, and the Internet.

Annie crawled from the tent, stood, and stretched. It was dusk, her favorite time of day.

Deputy Harris sat in a lawn chair nearby, texting on her iPhone.

"Are you going to get something to eat?" Annie asked.

The deputy looked up. "Somebody's supposed to bring me something pretty soon."

"I'm sorry to be so much trouble. I'm sure you've got better things to do."

"Not really. I kind of like it out here. So peaceful. And that tree. I've never seen anything quite like it. I want my children to see it. Kids these days, the only thing they want to look at is on the TV or the computer. 'Course, here I am with my iPhone."

"How many children do you have?"

"Two—a five-year-old boy and a seven-year-old girl. Jack and Sarah. How about you?"

"No kids. Just a cat. A very moody cat."

"Oh, well, I'm sorry. Uh, I mean..."

"I know what you mean. It's OK. Hey, what's that?"

Annie pointed across First Field. A flatbed truck was headed toward the bluff, hauling something tall and blue.

Deputy Harris stood up. A scratchy voice crackled from the radio attached to the shoulder of her uniform. "Deputy Harris?"

"Harris here."

"We've got a fella with a portable toilet on his way out there. Figured you might need it. He's bringing your dinner too. A plate from Bessinger's Barbecue. Hope that suits."

"Ten-four. Sounds good. I see him coming now. Thanks."

The truck, belonging to Johnny's Johnnies, pulled up beside the deputy. A man wearing a sweat-stained baseball cap that heralded Hambone's Bait and Tackle Shop leaned out of the driver-side window.

"Evenin', ma'am. Name's Johnny White. Johnny's Johnnies. I got a plate a food and a potty. Where you want the pot?"

"Wherever's easiest to put it. Long as it's not too far away."

Johnny handed the Styrofoam to-go plate to the deputy and turned to Annie. "They didn't give me nothing for you, ma'am. Hope you're doing OK."

"I've already eaten, so I'm good. How're you?"

"Fine as frog's hair, ma'am. Told the wife I was coming out here to deliver a potty and she said to make sure and get a picture of you and the tree. Would you mind? Hate to go home empty-handed."

"I don't mind, but the deputy might. Better ask her."

"Nope, sorry. Can't allow it. But once that toilet gets situated, I'm gonna be disappearing for a few minutes. Don't suppose I can control what happens while I'm indisposed."

"Gotcha." Johnny gave the deputy a thumbs-up. He wrestled the portable toilet to the ground and when the deputy went inside, he took a picture of Annie standing by the Old Lady.

"The wife said to tell you to stick to it, ma'am. Said ain't nobody got no business tearing down that pretty tree. I reckon I got to agree with her.

I ain't never seen nothing quite like it. I mean, it ain't even like a real tree. Like it's something bigger'n that. Something kinda magic-like, if you follow me."

"I follow you."

"And ma'am, I reckon it ain't none of my business, but don't go s'posing you're all by your lonesome out here. There's a dang three-ring circus out there by the gate. Everbody waving signs and whatnot. Radio stations setting up booths. Folks riding by honking horns. You done got folks worked into a real dither over this tree, and to my way of thinking, that ain't such a bad thing. Folks gotta care for something, else they wind up feeling for nothing, know what I mean?"

"I think I do."

"Well, ma'am, it's been mighty nice visiting with you. The wife says I talk too much, says I got more 'pinions than a porcupine's got quills, so I reckon I better hush up and be on my way. You hang in there, you hear?"

"Will do."

Johnny cranked his truck, waved good-bye, and drove away. Deputy Harris emerged from the portable toilet, buckling her thick belt. "Whew, that's better. Mrs. Hart, you're more than welcome to use it if you want."

"Thanks, but if I leave the tree, you're not going to do anything, are you?"

"Like what?"

"I don't know. I guess I just worry that some-body's going to try and get me away from it."

"Well, I'm sure not. We've got strict orders to leave you alone. Besides, nobody's got any business tearing that tree down anyway. Between you and me, I'm all for what you're doing. That tree really is the most amazing thing I've ever seen."

"It is amazing, isn't it?"

"Sure is. What kind of tree is it anyway?"

"She's a Southern live oak tree, several hundred years old."

"She?"

"I call her the Old Lady. She always seemed like a she to me."

"How'd you know she was out here?"

"It's a long story."

The deputy sat back in her lawn chair, rubbed her hands with a Handi Wipe, and opened the to-go plate. "I got all night to listen."

Two hours later, the sky had darkened, the stars had come out, the tree frogs were tuning up, and the two women were on a first name basis.

"Where'd you get the name Beanie?"

"First grade teacher said I was shaped like a butterbean. Been called Beanie ever since. How 'bout you? Is Annie short for something?"

"Annabelle. Never much liked it."

"Mmm. I can see what you mean. Sounds like an old-maid aunt you don't want to have to kiss when you're a kid. I had one of those. She always gave me a petticoat for Christmas. Annie suits you much better."

A comfortable silence settled between the two women. Beanie yawned, rubbed her eyes, and rose from her chair. "Time for me to turn in. It's been real nice talking to you. It's right brave what you're doing. Going up against these construction people and all. Not sure I could do it."

"But you're a cop."

"Yeah, but all I got is a badge and a gun. You're packing determination."

"Well, I hope it will be enough."

"Me too." The deputy folded her lawn chair. "I'm going to stretch out in the back of my patrol car. If you need anything, just give a holler, OK?"

"Will do. Goodnight. And Beanie?"

"Yeah?"

"It was good talking to you too."

Inside the tent, Annie nestled deep down in her sleeping bag. Lulled by the peace of the night and the shelter of the live oak, she closed her eyes, wondering if she really was packing enough determination to keep the Old Lady from harm.

She thought about Tom—how he remembered she loved Whopper Juniors but hated onions. How he was remarried, with a tow-headed child to boot. How she'd tried to be happy for him—managing it graciously on the outside, but much less gracefully on the inside.

Annie wondered if she, like her mother, was bound to die alone, snarled in a web of hospital sheets and unhappiness.

She envisioned her friends from so long ago, gathered in the branches of the Old Lady.

Annie wondered where they were, wishing they were here with her, and then, exhausted, she fell asleep.

Thunder wakes the night from its slumber. Annie has climbed high into the Old Lady. Branches creak as the wind and rain pick up. An explosive crack echoes across the landscape. Lightning strikes and a limb rips from the Old Lady's trunk, leaving a yellow gash that looks like an infected wound. Buck and Twig are racing across First Field. Ugly is a speck of frenetic white, charging ahead of them. "Buck! Twig!" Annie shouts, "I'm here! In the Old Lady!" But they do not hear her above the roil of the storm. They keep running. "Help! Her limbs are breaking!" she cries again, holding fast to the tree. Only Ugly stops. He is wet, panting. His nose, black and shiny as shoe polish, is poised in the air. He has caught the scent of Annie, the one who saved him. His bullet tail switches back and forth. "Com'on, Ugly!" Buck hollers, still running. Ugly whines, looks at Annie, and races after his master. Annie opens her mouth to shout for her friends once more, but nothing comes out. The storm ends as suddenly as it began. Buck, Twig, and Ugly vanish into the distance. And one by one, like soft feathers, the limbs of the Old Lady float to the earth without a sound.

"No," Annie murmured, "don't leave! The Old Lady needs..."

"Shh, Annie, I'm here. Be quiet or you'll wake the cop. Shh."

Annie roused herself. Was she dreaming? Was the Old Lady losing all her limbs? Was someone telling her to be quiet?

"Don't leave," she cried again.

"Dadgummit, Annie, wake up! Open your eyes!"

Annie felt strong hands grasping her shoulders. She opened her eyes and saw a handsome man with aquamarine eyes and close-cropped blonde hair. She turned his face, slowly to one side, so she could see the place just below his earlobe. Gently, she pressed her fingertip on a brown mole.

"Buck?"

"Yes, Annie, it's me. Buck."

"How in the world?" Annie propped herself up. "How'd you know where to find me? How'd you get here? There're cops at the gate. There's a deputy..."

"Shhh. She's asleep. I took a little detour getting here. Easy as pie. You sure as hell weren't hard to find, either. You're all over the news. People are talking about you everywhere. My office manager told me this morning there was some kooky lady on television who wasn't coming down out of a big live oak tree unless it was saved from destruc-tion. She said it was on a farm in Columbia, South Carolina, and she thought I might know where. Shoot, I didn't even have to wait for the next broadcast to know where. Or who. Hell, I knew it was you. I just knew it. So, I'm here to help. And I talked to Twig. He's on his way."

Annie stared at Buck. Her mouth had dropped open. Buck pushed it closed. Annie began to cry. Buck wrapped her in his arms. She felt his ropey muscles and his strength.

"It's OK, Annie. Really, it's OK."

Annie pushed Buck away from her.

"No, Buck, it's not OK. The baby. All these years I've tried not to think about it, about what we could have done, and what we should have done, but now, it's back. The whole thing. And I don't think I can handle it. I don't think I can stand to see the Old Lady pushed over either. Oh, God, what am I doing?"

"The right thing. Saving the Old Lady. She should never be harmed."

Buck pulled Annie back to him. He pressed his lips against her hair. "I've missed you," he murmured.

Annie pushed from him embrace. "Missed me?"

"Yes. *Missed you*. A lot."

"Are you flirting with me?"

"If you want to call it that."

"But..."

"But what?"

"But I don't know, Buck. A long time ago I thought maybe you liked me. Adolescent yearning, I suppose. But then, nothing ever materialized. And whatever it was your brother was talking about that you wrote in that diary. And then you never married."

"Do you think I'm gay?"

"Well, it wouldn't bother me if you were. My best friend is gay."

Buck looked at the tent ceiling and then back at Annie.

"What I wrote in that damn diary is that I felt confused and unsure of myself. Not sexually, but Jack interpreted it that way. It was typical, angst-ridden adolescent stuff. In fact, if you want to know the truth, Jack is the one who was uncertain of his sexuality. He came out a few years ago. He lives in Atlanta now, has a partner, is extremely happy. And I'm happy for him. He's a much nicer person being himself. But it took a long time for him to come to terms with things, and in the meantime, he foisted a lot of his feelings off on me. Only natural, I suppose, what with our father being so hard-edged and what with having a little brother to pick on. Believe me, I spent plenty of money with the therapist figuring out everything I've just told you in a couple of sentences. So..."

"So," Annie said, examining his left hand, which was rough but bare, "you're not married?"

"Nope. Never found the right lady. How about you?"

"Divorced. It sucks."

"I'm sorry. Kids?"

"No go. But let's don't go there. What about you? Where do you live? What are you doing?"

"Well, I never made it to med school, but I did make it to vet school. I have a large and small animal practice. I take care of critters. All sizes, sorts, and shapes. I live in Penland, North Carolina. Have a clinic and a house on top of a mountain. Clinic's nice, house is not much, but it works for me."

"Are you happy?"

"Not completely."

"Is anyone?"

"I don't suppose. So tell me, what are you doing with your life?"

"I'm an artist. Make sculptures out of found objects."

"Found objects?"

"Yep, stuff I find."

"Are *you* happy?"

"Sometimes, sometimes not. But really, the subject of me is a sore one. What about Twig and Briddy?"

"I've kept up with Twig some. He handles what few investments I have. He is—believe it or not—one hell of a high-powered investment broker. Lives in New York City and has more money than he knows what to do with."

"Really?"

"Yep, he's made a damn killing. He has a wife and a set of twins, a girl and a boy. As for Briddy, she's out in California. She runs a home for unwed mothers. Helps them have the babies. Helps them figure out what they want to do with the babies. Helps them get on with their lives."

"Wow."

"Yep, Twig said she's been pretty damned determined about things. Guess that's nothing new."

"Is she married? Any children of her own?"

"Don't think so."

"So when's Twig coming?"

"Probably on his way as we speak. Private jet, I'm sure."

Buck grabbed Annie's hand.

"Annie, I told you a lie a minute ago."

"A lie?"

"I did find the right lady, she just wasn't available by the time I figured it out."

"Who?"

Buck pulled Annie to his chest. "Who do you think?"

Annie and Buck lay in the tent, side by side. A crisp *snap* shook them from their embrace.

"What was that?" Annie whispered.

"Not sure." Buck reached for the opening of the tent. He unzipped it slowly, not making a sound.

"My God!"

"What?"

Buck turned to Annie, pressed his finger against his lips, and motioned her to the tent door. Annie looked out into the night. A spectacular buck, his head an altar of antlers, stared back at her.

"What's he doing?" Annie whispered.

"Probably hunting some Spanish moss. Whitetail love the stuff."

"He doesn't seem scared of us, does he?"

"Nope."

"How old do you think he is?"

"No telling."

The buck reached for a mouthful of moss and chewed it slowly. He looked at Annie and Buck once more, pawed the ground, snorted, and raced into the night.

"I guess we invaded his space," Annie said.

"He can share for one night," Buck replied.

CHAPTER SIXTEEN

Pilot Jim Thompson brought the twin-engine Citation in for an easy landing at Columbia Metropolitan Airport. Twig reached for his seat belt, unlatched it, and looked out the window. The iconic HOME OF THE FIGHTING GAMECOCKS sign—a neon-red relic of the early sixties—had disappeared from the rooftop of Eagle Aviation, a squat building not far from the main terminal.

Too bad, Twig thought to himself.

"Mr. Roebuck," Thompson announced, "we're in Columbia."

Twig looked at his watch—4:00 a.m.

Thompson eased the sleek jet to a stop in front of Eagle, where private airplanes came and went; the high keen of the Citation's engines waned and died. Twig stood, stretched his legs, and reached for his rucksack. Inside it was everything he thought he'd need, including his checkbook and a change of clothes.

"A car and driver should be waiting for you," said Mary Wooden, Twig's administrative assistant. "Are you sure you won't be needing my assistance?" Mary traveled everywhere with her employer.

"Nope, Mary, I'm on my own on this one. Keep your cell phone handy just in case, but you and Jim find a nice place to stay and relax. They say the Congaree Vista area is pretty nice these days. I'll be in touch. And don't forget

what I told you about Groucho's in Five Points.
Best deli around. Not to be missed."

"Yes, sir."

The black limousine pulled out of the airport
and headed for downtown Columbia. The
driver, in need of a shave, peered into his
rearview mirror. "So we're headed for the old
Montague farm out on Trenholm Road, is that
right?"

"Right. Know where it is?"

"My GPS does."

"Good."

Twig returned to his iPad, checking activity
in the overseas stock markets, but the limo
driver persisted.

"Now, is that the place where the lady is
camped out in the tree?"

"Yep."

"Damnedest thing I ever heard of. My wife says Geraldo's bound to show up. Says if he shows up, she's going out there to get his autograph. Me, I got my money on Oprah. So what're you? A TV reporter?"

"Nope, just a friend."

"Frienda who?" The driver scrutinized Twig.

"The tree."

"Hmph. Ain't never heard of a tree having so many friends."

The limo rolled through town. Twig checked his watch again—4:30 a.m. Forest Drive turned into Trenholm Road. At the intersection where he figured the top of Pine Tree Way should be located was an overbearing brick sign that said THE PRESERVE. Perfectly manicured bushes and a lush spread of marigolds surrounded a Cape-Cod-ish gatehouse.

"Jesus, things sure have changed around here," Twig mumbled.

"Sir?"

"Nothing. Just reminiscing to myself. When we get to the farm, don't pull over at the front gate. We'll go on past it, and I'll let you know where to stop."

"Yes, sir."

The limo passed by the gate. Several patrol cars were camped out at the entrance. A collection of signs was posted in the ground on the other side of the road. One said SAVE THE TREE, another HEY CONGAREE! CARE FOR MOTHER EARTH!

Twig directed the driver to stop underneath a stand of river birches. He loved the paper-thin curls of bark that covered the trees' trunks.

"Nobody needs to know you dropped me off here," he said, pressing a crisp $100 bill into the driver's hand.

"Yes, sir!" the driver replied. Twig grabbed his rucksack and closed the limo's heavy door as quietly as he could.

Twig examined his surroundings. He knew exactly where he was and where he was going. He grappled with the rusted barbed wire fence, scrambled through the woods, and located the farm road. He moved quickly down the dirt track, then found First Field which, though overgrown, remained wide, flat, and wondrous.

Twig stopped and breathed in the night air. His lungs filled with the sweet oxygen of venerable farmland. He wended his way through clumps of fescue, hogweed, and stinging nettle. He was grateful for canvas pants, hiking boots, and respites of wispy broom grass.

When Twig was able to discern the Old Lady's outline against the night sky, he was humbled. He stood in the field, mesmerized by the live oak. "You've grown, my old friend," he whispered.

Not far from the Old Lady, Twig spotted the police
car. Buck had told him to expect it. Twig turned
off his flashlight, gave the automobile a wide
berth, and stepped over the yellow tape. Benign
snoring emanated from a blue tent. Annie?
Buck? He would wake them in a minute, but first
he made his way to the Old Lady. He reached
out and touched her bark. It was rough and fur-
rowed. Moved in a way he had not expected,
drawn in by the undertow of his childhood, Twig
spread his arms around her and wept.

"I missed you," he cried softly. A gentle wind
stirred among the Old Lady's long, leathery
leaves.

Twig gathered himself, turned, and made his
way back through the maze of raised, woody
roots that anchored the Old Lady to the earth. He
stooped in front of the tent and quietly unzipped
the flap door. Buck was the one snoring, wrapped
in a blanket and nestled against Annie. She was
bundled up inside a sleeping bag.

Twig squeezed the top of her foot. "Annie."

She opened her eyes and smiled. "Twig," she whispered softly. "I'm so glad you're here."

"Me, too."

"Come in. You look tired. I mean, you look wonderful, but tired."

"I guess I didn't get much sleep. Must've been journey proud, you know?"

"Yeah, I know."

Annie hugged Twig long and hard, surprised by the breadth of his chest. He no longer seemed so fragile. She moved to make room for him in the cramped space. Buck opened his eyes. He sat up, still wrapped in his blanket.

"Hey, buddy, welcome aboard." The two men shook hands.

"Is the cop still asleep?" Buck asked Twig.

"Like a baby," Twig said. "So this is a good time to talk. I've got something I need to tell y'all before that cop wakes up, before anything else happens out here."

Buck and Annie stared at their old friend.

Twig drew a deep breath. "A long time ago, I told y'all a lie. A big lie. The baby wasn't dead. When I went back to the farm, it was alive."

"Oh, Jesus," Annie gasped. "Please don't tell me anymore. Just don't tell me."

Buck grasped Annie's hand and looked at Twig. "You told us the baby was dead. You told us you buried it."

"I had to promise Naomi..."

"Naomi?" Annie asked.

"I took the baby to Naomi."

Buck looked at Annie and then back at Twig. "You took the baby to Naomi? All the way across town? In a frigging snowstorm?"

"Yes, I did." Twig turned to Annie. "Do you remember when we left the farm that afternoon? You and me? Buck made us go home, remember?"

"Yes," Annie whispered.

"And we got to the barbed wire fence and you went to your house, right? And then later that night—much later—I showed up underneath your bedroom window and told you not to worry, I had gone back to the farm and there was nothing we could've done to save the baby, that it really was dead? Well, that was a lie. A real big one. The baby was alive."

Annie stared at Twig. Her eyes grew steely. Silence filled the tent.

"Please say something, *anything*," Twig pleaded.

"OK," Annie snapped, "I will. You know what I did after you stood under my window and told me that baby was dead? I proceeded to base my whole stupid life on the shitty fact that even though I didn't believe you—that surely we could've done something to help the baby, *should've done something*, that we basically killed that little boy—it was OK. OK, except I wound up feeling like I didn't deserve to have my own baby. So fuck you and your lie, Twig."

"Annie, please..."

"No, don't you dare 'please' me! Do you know that when I was married I got pregnant once and that ended in a miscarriage? A miscarriage, I should add, that I was happy about. I flushed a fetus down the toilet—*my tiny baby*—and I was fucking *relieved*. I felt like I had paid my dues. Tit for tat, for God's sake, and I'm not even the guilt-ridden Catholic here. And now, after all this time, you're telling me the baby lived? Jesus, I gotta get out of here."

Annie lunged for the tent door. Twig reached for her.

"No," Buck said, "let her go."

Annie climbed into the Old Lady. As high as she could go. Fury fed her muscles. Her hands found every successive branch, her bare feet, every toehold. When she reached a safe, high place, she stopped. The wind blew through her hair; hot tears rolled down her face.

Below her, Buck stood on a thick branch. "Annie, I'm sorry. Twig's sorry too, real sorry. But please, come down. We've got to get this thing figured out, and fast."

"What's to figure out?" Annie stared out over the horizon of the bluff. Safelight—the rosy color of dawn—was on its way.

"How we're going to save the Old Lady. Twig has a plan. You need to hear it."

"What I need is to start my life over. Does Twig have a plan for that?"

"Annie, for God's sake, I understand you're mad as hell but we've got to talk. All of us.

Please come down. Not for me, not for Twig, and not for you. But for the Old Lady. *Please?*"

Back inside the tent, Twig chose his words carefully. He trained his eyes on Annie.

"OK, the baby was born alive. Tiny, but alive. When I went back to the barn, Buck was huddled up against a post, holding the baby and crying because he didn't know what to do with it. At that point, I don't know if he knew the baby was alive or dead. I think he just knew he didn't know *what* to do. But he did know Briddy couldn't keep it. He was just sitting there, rocking the baby back and forth. Briddy was asleep. I told Buck to give me the baby and that I would take care of things. I told him to take Briddy home, and that's what he did."

Twig looked at Buck. "Right so far?"

"Right."

"So then I took the baby to Naomi."

"How in the world did you do that?" Annie asked.

"Well, I prayed to Saint Christopher for a safe journey, wrapped the baby up inside my jacket, and I started walking. When I got to the shopping center, there was a man in a utility truck. I swear to God, I think he was an angel. He rolled his window down and asked me if I needed a ride somewhere. I said yes, and he took me all the way to Naomi's."

Buck looked skeptical. "He didn't ask any questions? Like what the hell was a scrawny kid like you doing out in the middle of a snowstorm?"

"Not one single question. I'm telling y'all, he was an angel."

Annie looked at Twig, amazed. "So that's why Naomi quit working for us so suddenly?"

"That's exactly right. She left town with the baby."

"But where'd she go?" Annie asked.

It was like Christmas, having a day off from work during the week. Mrs. Mackey had called early to say that the buses were not running, that it would be impossible for Naomi to get to Shimmering Pines.

Naomi spent the first part of the morning wrapped in her covers in her bed, watching the snow fall. Snow was a magical thing; it had the capacity to make even an ugly place like the Bottom look pretty. She wondered what the old Montague farm must look like—it was bound to be a spectacular sight. She knew the children would be out there all day.

Later in the morning, Lily arrived on Naomi's front porch, stomping the snow off her boots. The two friends took a walk in the neighborhood, watching delighted children use anything they could find to slide in the snow. The youngsters wore socks on their hands and bags over the shoes on their feet.

Later, Naomi invited Lily to her house for hot chocolate and an early dinner of chili, beans, and cornbread. It had been a perfect, unexpected kind of day, and after Lily left, Naomi had gone to bed.

At first, she thought she was dreaming. No one ever knocked on her door so late at night. If it had been Lily, she would've called first. The knocking was persistent, needy. Naomi put on her terry bathrobe and slippers. She tiptoed through the small house, careful not to make noise or turn on lights. She reached a window near the front door and peered out. There, on the front stoop, stood Twig. He was wearing a heavy coat, much too big for him. His arms were wrapped around his middle, as if he were carrying something inside the coat. Twig reached out to knock on the door again, but Naomi opened it before he could make any more noise.

"What in the world are you doing here?" she demanded. Twig's face was red and chapped.

"I-I-I got something for you," he stuttered, barely able to talk.

"Well, for heaven's sake, child, get inside this house."

Twig stepped across the threshold. Naomi looked up and down the street and then closed the door. She turned to Twig. "Now I'm going to ask you again, what in the world are you doing here? It's the middle of the night. It's freezing cold. How'd you get...?"

"I brought you something," he said, sitting on the floor and gently retrieving the bundle from inside his coat. "You gotta take it, Naomi. Here, you just gotta take it."

"What is it?" She stared at the tight swaddling of an old sweatshirt in Twig's lap.

Twig pulled back a corner of the gray material. "It's a baby. A little baby boy, just like I said I'd get you if I could."

Naomi's heart jumped. She stepped back, covered her mouth, and then stepped forward again, frightened but intrigued. The infant's eyes were closed. His hair was dark and curly. His skin, the color of coffee ice cream.

"My God, young man, where in the world did this child come from?"

"Briddy. Briddy had a baby. She had it in the barn at the farm this afternoon. Terrence, you know, the colored boy, he's the daddy. Briddy, Buck, and Annie think the baby died and that I buried it. But it was alive. It's tiny, and I think it came too early, but it's alive, and you gotta take it. Please, Naomi, you know Briddy can't keep a baby. Especially a colored one."

"Oh, Jesus," Naomi cried, sinking to her knees, sitting beside Twig.

Twig put the bundle in Naomi's lap. The infant's eyes opened and then closed again.

"Has he had anything to eat?"

"Not as far as I know."

"Oh, dear, sweet Jesus in Heaven, he needs to eat. He needs something to eat."

Naomi stood from the floor and went into the kitchen. She cast about inside the refrigerator and then remembered that Lily had baby formula at her house. Lily had found a stray kitten a week ago and was feeding it the formula from a tiny bottle.

"Twig, I want you to go to Lily's house. It's just up the street. On the right. Number twenty. She has one of those concrete jockey statues out front, the face is painted white. Knock on the door, wake her up, tell her to bring the baby formula and come here, to my house. Tell her we need her help. And hurry."

Twig took the steps down Naomi's porch two at a time and ran into the dark. Naomi carried the baby into the kitchen. She sat in Grandee's chair, holding the infant against her chest, humming with the back and forth rhythm of the old rocker.

Twig returned with Lily in minutes. Lily had the small bottle and the formula. Without saying a word, she heated the milky liquid in a pot on the stove, poured it into the bottle, and gave it to Naomi. Naomi offered the bottle to the child. It sucked hungrily.

"Praise the Lord," Lily whispered. "Look what he done did now."

The three sat quietly in the kitchen while the baby sucked on the bottle. When the child had finished, Naomi lifted it to her shoulder, patted its tiny back, and a small burp came forth.

"You were meant to have this baby," Lily announced. "Twig done told me most of the story."

"Lily, I can't possibly keep this child. You know that. It's bound to be against the law. It's bound to be..."

"Girl, it ain't bound to be nothing but your baby."

"Please, Naomi, you just have to keep it," Twig pleaded.

"But *how*?" Naomi asked.

"Ain't you still got your Grandee's little place over in McCormick?" Lily asked.

"I do, but..."

"But nothing, girl. Just go. Tomorrow. Whenever we can get you there. I'll help you. I'll call Mrs. H and tell her I'm taking a week off. I'll make up something. My mama's sick and I have to tend to her. Anything."

"She'll fire you."

"No, she won't. She needs me too bad to do that. She's gonna be president of some fancy women's club next year and she's already planning all the teas she's gonna have at her house. Girl, she ain't gonna be able to do without me."

"But what about this place? And my job with the Mackeys? And a birth certificate..."

"And *nothing*, girl," Lily countered. "You can rent this place. Shoot, I'll move from where I am to here. I'll rent it from you. I like it a whole lot better than my place. As for the Mackeys, call Mrs. Mackey and tell her you're quitting. She don't need no explanation other than she's home and you ready to go back to school. And a birth certificate? You and me go downtown to wherever we got to go to. We get dressed kinda shabby-like and tell 'em it was a at-home birthin'. Show 'em the baby, tell 'em you the mama and I witnessed the birthing. Then I'll whisper all contrite-like that they ain't no daddy to be signing the birth certificate. They'll believe it comin' out two poor-lookin' colored women's mouths."

"How do you know?"

" 'Cause white folk *wants* to believe stuff like that. That's how I know."

The baby yawned; the inside of his mouth was the color of a pink rosebud.

"But what am I going to live on?"

"For right now, that money you've got saved up for college. You're always talking about that money you got saved up. Time to use it, girl. And once you get settled, you can find something to do. You can take care of somebody else's baby. In your house. Get paid for that. Just don't try to figure it all out at once. Just trust that things will work out. Put it in God's hands, girl. He already done put a baby in yours."

"But what about Annie?"

"Annie's got her mama back," Twig offered. "She'll be fine."

"Then what about Briddy? This is her child. And the father..."

"He don't know nothing about it," Twig said. "Shoot, he's gone back to New Jersey. And Briddy, well, she thinks the baby was born dead. That's just as well, don't you think? 'Cause she sure can't keep it."

"Naomi," Lily said, putting a hand on her friend's shoulder, "Twig's right. Someday, girl, maybe everyone can know the truth. And maybe it'll be all right for a white girl to have a half-colored baby. But not now. Not right now. Think what would happen to Briddy if her mama finds out she done had a baby. A colored one. And God knows what would happen to the baby. Jesus, girl, *think*."

Naomi looked at the baby. The child opened its eyes and returned her gaze, kindling a fire long left unlit in her heart.

"Well," Naomi whispered, "he needs a name."

"So where is Naomi now?" Annie asked Twig.

"And the baby?" Buck added.

"Naomi's right there at her Grandee's old place in McCormick. The baby—well, I guess he's a grown man by now."

"Does Briddy know?" Annie asked. "Does she know she has a son?"

"She does. I told her a long time ago, but as far as I know, they've never met. I think Briddy wanted her privacy. She didn't want to confuse the boy, and in the long run, I think she felt like Naomi shouldn't have to share her motherhood."

"Does Naomi know about all this? I mean, what's happening right now, with the Old Lady?"

"Yep, I called her."

"But what about the Old Lady? If push came to shove, we were going to force the preservation of the tree because of the burial site. Now what?"

Twig looked at Annie and Buck. "I prayed to Saint Jude and I've got it all figured out."

CHAPTER SEVENTEEN

Buck and Twig crept out of the tent. Gray-pink light, like the color inside an oyster shell, was slipping over the horizon.

"We'll see you in a little while," Buck assured Annie.

"But what if they don't let you back on the property? Why can't y'all just stay?"

Twig put his hand on Annie's shoulder; they'd managed enough of a truce to focus on the Old

Lady's future. "Trust me, they'll let us back on the property. Money works wonders, but annoying the cops by being here wouldn't be helpful."

"OK, but swear you'll be back?"

"Swear it," Buck promised with a fist bump.

"And you've got Tom's cell phone number?" Annie asked Twig.

"Got it. As soon as I get a signal, I'm calling him."

Annie kneeled at the tent door. She watched the friends disappear into First Field. One followed the other; if she squinted her eyes, making the field's tawny colors mix, the scene looked like a Wyeth painting.

Annie's attention turned to a pair of rowdy blue jays. They were harassing a squirrel foraging for acorns among the Old Lady's roots. Annie had read somewhere that the live oak's acorns were particularly sweet, that they fed not only squirrels but deer, wood ducks, quail, and raccoons. She also knew that the tree's wood was hard, strong, and prized among shipbuilders of long ago.

"A provider," Annie said out loud. "That's what you are."

"Good morning!" Beanie's sudden voice startled Annie. "Sorry, didn't mean to scare you. Sleep good?"

"I did. How about you?"

"Remarkably well for the back of a police cruiser. Had breakfast?"

"A cereal bar."

"Well, my buddies at the gate radioed to say they're bringing us some sausage biscuits and hot coffee. How does that sound?"

"Wonderful."

By 9:00 a.m., a crowd had gathered near the Old Lady—Tom, his paralegal, several Congaree attorneys and executives, Solicitor Barnes, Sheriff Babson, a representative of the South Carolina Nature Conservancy, and Twig and Buck, who had joined Annie as Tom's clients.

Tom asked to speak with Annie, Twig, and Buck. Alone, in the tent.

The Congaree attorneys protested. Sheriff Babson waved them off and looked at Tom. "Five minutes, then we're getting this show on the road."

Tom, Twig, and Buck crossed the yellow tape and joined Annie in the tent.

"So," the attorney began, "here's the latest. Henry Porter is on his way as we speak."

"*The* Henry Porter?" Annie asked.

"Yep, the Henry Porter."

"I've read about him," Twig said. "Sounds like a pretty interesting guy."

"He'll never win," Buck announced.

"I beg your pardon," Annie countered.

"Hey," Tom cautioned, "we haven't got time for political bickering."

"Do you really think he can be helpful?" Twig asked Tom.

"Actually, I think he might be. Right now, his campaign is mired down in who his parents are. He's not said. I suppose he's an illegitimate child, and I suppose there's an argument to be made that whomever had him should not be made a matter of public knowledge, but still, the Republicans are going crazy and the press is getting antsy. Porter's a political animal. Smart as hell. But he also seems to be a pretty sincere fellow in some respects. He's an ardent environmentalist. He does a lot of hiking, bird-watching. That kind of thing. Apparently he's particularly worried about global warming. In any case, he might just have a real interest in saving this tree. I haven't talked to him, but it might be that the burial site issue can remain just that—buried."

Buck, Annie, and Twig looked at one another.

Annie pointed at Twig. "You tell him."

"There's no baby buried here."

Tom looked at the threesome. He took his glasses off, rubbed his eyes, and put the glasses back on.

"You know, guys, it's not every day that I get to represent a lovely lady and friend who has climbed into a tree and vows not to come down until it is saved from destruction. Certainly, it's not every day that I'm asked to protect a burial site and then am told there is no such thing. And while I have actually enjoyed the time I've spent on this case, which is a rarity these days, it's time to cut to the chase. Now,

Solicitor Barnes could bob around here forever, basking in the publicity, but Congaree
Development is running out of patience. So is
Sheriff Babson. And never mind Henry Porter,
who is on his merry way. Consequently, in the
next few minutes, I want the whole truth and
nothing but the truth, so help you God and this
damn tree. Got it?"

"Got it," Buck, Twig, and Annie replied in
unison.

Twig told Tom the story of the baby being taken
to Naomi. When he had finished the tale, Tom
closed his folder.

"You know, if it wasn't for growing up in the early
sixties in the South myself, I would not believe
this story. But I do. Amazing. Just because I'm
curious, has anyone been in touch with Naomi
lately? I'm assuming she's still alive?"

"She's still alive," Twig said. "I talked to her
when all this started. She wants us to go see
her when this is all over."

"Well, for God's sake, don't do that. The miracle of this situation, other than a teenager was able to hide a pregnancy and that four kids were able to successfully birth a baby in a barn during a snowstorm, is that this story has remained under wraps all this time. We need to keep it that way, so the last thing anybody needs to do is go trotting over to McCormick and open up the possibility that some inspired reporter gets the scent of a bigger story and finds its trail."

"OK," Annie said.

"Mr. Hart, your five minutes is up." It was Sheriff Babson.

Tom poked his head out of the tent. "Just five more, please?"

"Make it snappy," the sheriff grumbled.

"So, now, let's back up," Tom said. "We need to rethink a few things. And fast."

"Tom," Twig said, "I have a plan."

"Shoot."

"I own a pretty sweet stretch of property along the Congaree River, in the Congaree Vista. Bought it many years ago as an investment. Couldn't see how that land wouldn't eventually become a no-brainer for upscale commercial or residential development. Anyway, I'm willing to make a trade with Congaree. I'll give them the deed to the riverfront property if Congaree will give me a quarter acre surrounding, and obviously including, the Old Lady, with the understanding that I will turn that deed over to the South Carolina Nature Conservancy, which will be responsible for caring for the Old Lady to the end of her lifetime. I have already had my people talk to the Conservancy—they have a representative here—and they are on board. Now if Congaree doesn't like that idea, I have another plan."

'What's that?" Tom asked.

"I will file as many lawsuits *against* Congaree and *for* the Old Lady as my legal team can come up with. I will make sure Congaree is gummed up in court for a good, long time—this development project will be dead in the water."

Annie stared at Twig. She was spellbound.

"Sorry," Twig said to her. "I know I sound nasty, but that's the nature of business these days. When you get pushed, you push back fast and a whole lot harder. In this case, however, I think it's one hell of a deal for Congaree. They can still build condos out here and they'll have the riverfront property too."

Tom rubbed his brow again. "I don't know. I'm just not sure..."

Tom was interrupted by a voice outside the tent.

"Mr. Hart?"

"Yes?"

"This is Henry Porter. Might you be so kind as to poke your head out here for a minute?"

Tom gave Annie, Buck, and Twig a thumbs-up. He hurried to his feet and scrambled out of the tent.

"Welcome to our neck of the woods, Mr. Porter. I'm Tom Hart, representing Annie Hart, Twig Roebuck, and Buck McCain. I'm glad to see you..."

Porter was dressed in khakis, a yellow oxford shirt, and a blue blazer. He was tall and fit. His teeth were straight and white, his eyes were green, his skin was paper-bag brown.

"Mr. Hart, would you ask your clients to come outside please?"

"Certainly."

"I'm planning on voting for you," Annie said, smiling and introducing herself.

"Sorry, North Carolina resident," Buck offered, shaking Porter's hand.

"The great state of New York," Twig added, extending his hand too.

An hour later, a press conference was held underneath the Old Lady. Porter spoke slowly and eloquently.

"As you may know, I am a proponent of the environment. I feel quite strongly that every human inhabitant of this earth must do what he or she can to protect the place that is our home, our sustenance, our very life. With that in mind, I am intrigued by the beauty of this Southern live oak tree that we are all now standing underneath. This tree is not only a magnificent representation of her species, but she is also a contributor to the quality of our environment. Many things could have gone wrong between now, as we stand here, and the time when this tree was a mere small seedling hundreds of years ago. She has surely survived many things—droughts, pestilence, fires, storms—but most of all, she has survived us. *People.* And now she faces her toughest enemy again. But let us be her friend. Let this tree stand today as testimony not only to the strength and endurance of nature, but to the necessity that we, as human beings, respect and protect nature's gifts."

Porter paused and looked into the branches of the Old Lady.

"Far be it for me to know these things, but I would suspect that this tree has a certain kind of wisdom—having lived through generations of people, through annals of history—that we, as relatively short-lived beings in comparison, will never have. With that said, I am pleased to announce that this Southern live oak tree will not be destroyed. I have discussed this situation with all parties involved, and we have been able to reach an agreement that is satisfactory to everyone concerned. The tree will be left undisturbed. Congaree Development will be remunerated by an anonymous donor for the loss of this small, albeit valuable, piece of property. That donor will be given a deed to the small portion of property, which will then be turned over to the South Carolina Nature Conservancy. The Conservancy has agreed to care for the live oak through the duration of its natural life. When the tree dies, of natural causes, the property will remain in the hands of the Conservancy and another live oak will be planted in its place."

Porter gazed at the people gathered around him.

"I would like to thank Congaree Development for its flexibility in this matter. And I would like to thank Mrs. Annie Hart, and her friends, Buck McCain and Twig Roebuck, who together spent many years as children climbing in this tree, for their determination to do something right. We all should have such determination. Now, if there are any questions, I will be happy to answer them."

"Mr. Porter?" asked a woman with a reporter's notebook in her hand.

"Yes, ma'am, go ahead."

"There have been recent rumors that you are the child of..."

"Excuse me, Ms.—?"

"Wise. Diane Wise. WIS-TV."

"Ms. Wise, I came here to discuss a tree. A beautiful, valuable old tree. I am happy that we have been able to save it from destruction. I am not happy that the matter seems of little or no consequence to you. As I have said before, I will not discuss who my mother and father are. I will say this, however, which is more than I have said before. My natural parents are not criminals. They are not two- or three-headed. They are simply two people, who at a very tender and young time in their lives, did not intend to have a baby. To invade their privacy would be a crime, as far as I am concerned, and as much as I can, I will not allow it."

"But are you going to release your birth certificate to..."

Porter grimaced.

"This press conference is over," he said, walking away from the microphone and disappearing into a big, dark automobile.

By late afternoon, the appropriate legal papers had been drawn up and signed. The media had left to file stories.

Tom shook Buck and Twig's hands and turned to leave.

"I'll walk you to the car," Annie said.

After he opened the Land Rover door, Tom turned to Annie. "Well, I guess that's it. One very pretty tree saved. Back to much more mundane work."

Annie reached for Tom's hand. "There is nothing I can say that will thank you enough for what you have done in the last two days. It has meant the world to me. It's just that I wish..."

"Annie, please..."

"No, Tom, let me talk. I need to say this. I need to tell you how much I loved you and how much I still do. You gave me so much, and I gave you so little. I'm sorry for that. So sorry for that, but I don't think I could have done otherwise. People talk about unconditional love all the time, but I don't know what that is. I'm not sure I ever will, and I'm sorry to have put you through my perversity. I'm sorry I couldn't open my whole heart to you. It makes me sick."

"Annie, for God's sake, it wasn't just you. No matter what, it takes two to tango. I should've looked deeper into your heart and seen the sadness. I didn't."

Annie pressed her head against Tom's chest. "Friends?" she murmured.

"Friends," Tom replied, lifting Annie's chin. "Now listen to me. Your friend, the vet?"

"Yeah?"

"He's all about you."

"What do you mean?"

"I mean he's in love with you."

"Really?"

"Does a bear shit in the woods? Yeah, really. There was hardly room enough for all of us inside that tent. He's a nice guy, Annie. A real nice guy. Try opening your heart the whole way this time, OK? Just try."

Tom stepped inside the Rover, cranked it, and drove away, waving out the window as he went.

Annie turned toward those still gathered at the Old Lady. She thanked the developers again for their patience and asked if, by any chance, she, Buck, and Twig could spend one more night on the farm.

Miraculously, they said yes.

CHAPTER EIGHTEEN

nnie and Twig sat cross-legged on the ground near the Old Lady. Buck put the finishing touches on a campfire and leaned over to light it. The fire caught quickly and began to crackle. The three had spent the afternoon exploring the farm. Dorsey talked his way through a single deputy still stationed at the farm's front gate and had delivered several bottles of chilly Dom Perignon and deli sandwiches to the campers.

"So Twig," Buck said, sitting back, "when're you headed home?"

"Tonight."

"Tonight?" Annie asked. "That's crazy. Stay here. We've got permission."

"Real life beckons," Twig replied.

"What time's your flight?"

"Whatever time he wants it to be," Buck laughed.

Twig looked sheepish.

"Ohhh," Annie smiled, "I remember. You've got a private airplane. Or is it a jet?"

"A small jet. A Citation."

"The only citation I have is stuck to my refrigerator door. It's from the City of Columbia for parking in a loading zone the other day. So, you've really done well for yourself, haven't you?"

"Yeah, I guess you could say I have." Twig poked the fire with a stick.

"Nothing wrong with that," Buck offered.

"I'm not saying anything's wrong with it," Annie countered, "but the last time we spent any time together, Twig was hoping to be a saint. What happened to those plans?"

"Funny you should ask, because I've been thinking about it a lot lately. Do you remember that plan Naomi created for me to quit pissing in my pants and sheets? Well, it was a real eye-opener."

"How so?" Buck asked.

"I really got into it. Not just the fact that the plan really did help me break my habit, but I started creating graphs and timelines to analyze my progress. Rather than just hoping or praying for a remedy, the graphs and lines made real sense to me. I guess they offered me a concrete path instead of a pipe dream. I showed them to Naomi one day, and she said I was bound to be a businessman when I grew up. She said I had a way with numbers, and I guess I did."

"That's amazing," Buck said.

"But I'll tell you this," Twig replied, raising his glass of champagne, "I haven't abandoned my saints, and I'll be saying a prayer to Saint Bibiana tonight."

"What his story?" Buck asked.

"*She* takes care of hangovers."

The friends laughed and the fire blazed.

Annie looked at Twig. "So tell us about Briddy. Do you ever see her? Hear from her?"

"Occasionally, we get together. But not often. There was a period of time when we saw a lot of each other—several years ago—when both Mom and Dad got sick. They died within a year of each other, and after that, Briddy had no real reason to come east. So she stays out west. If you recall, she was always determined as hell, and one thing she was absolutely deter- mined about after Mom and Dad died was to put that part of her life behind her. You know, no matter what it was, she'd toss that heavy mane of red hair over her shoulders and never look back. So, I think she's happy."

"Well, good for her," Annie said. "It sounds like you haven't looked back either. Sounds like you're real happy, too."

"I am. Jill's a wonderful wife and mother. The twins, the family, it means everything. But enough about me, how 'bout you guys? Annie, I know you and Tom got a divorce. He seems like a nice guy. That must have been tough."

"It was, but I'm still here, all in one piece."

"What about your mom and dad?"

"Mom died a while back. Dad lives at an Episcopal retirement home in West Columbia. It's a lovely old place. He has a small cottage. He has Alzheimer's too, but there's a wonderful lady named Delores who takes care of him."

"Ever think you'll get married again?"

"Me? I doubt it."

The fire was burning lower. Buck added a few branches to it.

Twig turned his questions to Buck. "What about your parents?"

"Mom's in Richmond, Virginia. Lots of family up there. She's in pretty good shape, but she can't take care of Dad anymore. He's in a VA nursing home, in a wheelchair. Spends his days rehashing life in the military with the rest of the old soldiers."

"So I think I heard you say Jack is gay. How'd your parents deal with his coming out? I'm assuming he did do that—come out, I mean."

"Mom struggled—wondered what she'd done wrong. Then she came to terms with it. Dad, on the other hand, doesn't know. He'd go ballistic if he did."

"What about you? How do you feel about it?"

"Suits me fine. Like I told Annie, he's a lot nicer person these days. We see each other every couple of weeks. He brings his partner up to the mountain. Nice guy."

The three friends were quiet. Twig stood up, stretched his arms toward the indigo sky, and turned to Annie and Buck. "Would y'all ever believe that we'd wind up together underneath the Old Lady after so long?"

The magnificent tree stood out against the dark horizon.

"Amazing, isn't it?" Buck said. "I mean, we saved her. We did exactly what Twig told Mr. Montague we'd do. I'll never forget that day, you standing there in front of that man, your feet planted in the dirt like they had roots."

"Well, I meant what I said to him. But the thing is, looking back on it all, I think the Old Lady sort of saved us too."

"How so?" Annie asked.

"Well, hell, she protected us. We sought her shelter, whether it was from too much sun or too much meanness in people. We always came here, to her. I don't know about y'all, but the Old Lady certainly did more to comfort and care for me than my mother or father ever did. I mean, don't you feel like she has a soul of some kind? It's like what Porter was talking about—a kind of wisdom that we humans can't possibly have? Something that comes with living for generations. Interesting stuff. Makes me think those people who talk to houseplants aren't all that nuts."

An owl hooted in the distance.

"Well, guys," Twig said, looking at his watch, "my ride's probably waiting for me at the gate. Group hug before I go?"

"You really have to leave?" Annie asked.

"Afraid so."

The threesome embraced.

"There's one more thing I need to say while we're all here together," Annie said.

"What's that?" Twig asked.

"Well, it's just that I'm sorry we lost contact with each other. We were such good friends and then we weren't friends anymore. That seems so impossible, but I guess I was just so angry and scared after the baby was born, and then Mom got sick again and I went off to boarding school..."

"It wasn't just you and boarding school," Buck said to Annie. "Shoot, we moved to Richmond. I mean, really, Twig and Briddy were the only ones of us left in the neighborhood and maybe that wasn't such a bad thing."

Twig grasped Annie's shoulder. "The truth is, I think time was the only friend we had after all that happened. And she was a good friend. She brought us to where we are now, and that's a good place, don't you think?"

"Yeah," Annie murmured, "I do."

Twig turned toward First Field. Annie and Buck watched his silhouette disappear into the distance and then sat by the fire again.

"Annie?"

"Hmm?"

"Would you come visit me in North Carolina? I'd love to show you around the mountain. I think you'd love it there. A long weekend, something like that?"

Annie looked hard at Buck.

"Why are you looking at me like that?"

"I don't know. Maybe I'm scared again."

"Of what?"

"Us."

"Jesus, Annie, I don't want to scare you. I want to love you."

"You do? You really do?"

"I really do."

"Can I think about it? The long weekend, I mean?"

"Think all you want, but do me a favor."

"What's that?"

"After you've finished thinking, after you've got it all figured out, listen to that thing that beats inside you. Listen to your heart and let go."

"Of what?"

"Of everything but right now. Of everything but the rest of your life."

CHAPTER NINETEEN

The trip to McCormick was not a long one, but long enough for Annie to think about things. She often did her best thinking in the car, when no one was with her and the countryside rolled by in green and brown waves. Mostly brown, now that it was early November.

Annie smiled as the Jeep bumped along.

It had been a remarkable several days spent with childhood friends she'd always assumed she'd never see again. Annie was always

trying to come up with the next idea for a good
reality television show, and she thought bringing long-lost childhood friends back together
might be a darn good one.

Twig had e-mailed to say that he wanted her
and Buck to gather with him for a New Year's
celebration in the city. He said Jill would love
to have a reason to entertain, and so they had
agreed that they would do that. Twig said he
would send the Citation to pick them up.

When Annie had finally gotten home from the
farm, all her mailboxes were full—telephone,
e-mail, and snail mail. A telephone call from
the editor of the Nature Conservancy magazine
was the only one she returned immediately.
The editor wanted to do a story about the Old
Lady early next year. Would Annie agree to be
interviewed? She said she would think about it.

Annie had also gone to see her father as soon
as she could. Delores had called to say that he
had been very aware of what was going on dur-

ing the fight to save the Old Lady and that he was determined to go see the tree.

When Annie and her father arrived at the farm, where work had begun in earnest, they were met by Mr. Dempsey.

"Well, what the..." he said, smiling when he saw Annie. "If it ain't the tree-saving lady. You shore got it done, didn't you?"

"Well, *we* got it done. It wasn't just me, it was a lot of us, really. This is my father, Jim Mackey. Daddy, this is Mr. Dempsey. He runs the bulldozers."

"Nice to meet you, sir," Mr. Dempsey said, shaking the elderly man's hand. "You got yourself quite a daughter here."

Mr. Mackey nodded, a faint smile crossed his face.

"So how is she?" Annie asked.

"She?"

"The Old Lady."

"Oh, yes, the tree. Well, she's fine and dandy. Sitting just as pretty as you please on top of that bluff. Damn near looks like a queen. Wanna take your dad to see her? I was headed that way myself, and I got plenty of room in my truck. Why don't y'all just ride with me?"

Annie led her father to the big, double-cab truck. "Sorry for the mess," Mr. Dempsey said, shoving empty paper coffee cups and invoices aside. Annie slid into the middle of the bench seat. She reached her hand out to her father who climbed in beside her. The truck rattled across the landscape.

"One day they may put a real road out here," Mr. Dempsey shouted above the noise of the truck's progress. "Now that tree, it's done made this place famous. They can't sell the condos fast enough, especially the ones 'round the bluff."

"They're not bothering the tree, are they?" Annie asked, concerned.

"Heck, no. She's the dadgum draw. Developers can't build as many condos, but what they can build are selling like high-priced hotcakes. That tree makes for a spectacular sight, especially at night. They already done run some ground lights in there so she looks real pretty in the dark."

"Lights?"

"Now, don't you worry none, Mrs. Hart, we're following all the rules and regulations, and that nature group's like a dog on a bone. They got somebody out here every day making sure it's all done right. That tree is gonna be just fine. Hell, she's gonna be the best taken care of tree there ever was."

"Well, that's good."

And it was. Annie and her father spent a few minutes at the Old Lady. A handsome split-rail fence had been erected in a large square around the area. The Old Lady stood gracefully at its center. Annie showed her father where First Field was and where they would have walked across from the old neighborhood, Shimmering Pines. Mr. Dempsey then took them back to Annie's Jeep, but not before Annie kissed the trunk of the Old Lady.

"You love that old tree," Annie's father declared.

"Yes, Daddy, I do."

The elderly man's eyes focused on Annie.

"I love you. Your mother would be proud."

"You think so?"

Annie's father struggled to find the words he wanted. "She...she...she loved you. But she didn't lose you like she lost that boy. She...she never had to miss you and grieve for you the way she had to for that boy."

A tear trickled down his wrinkled face. "What was that boy's name? He loved baseball."

Annie pulled her father to her. "Will," she whispered.

His shoulders sagged in her arms. "Daddy, it's OK."

He pulled away from her. "I'm glad she came home, aren't you?"

"Came home? You mean from the place in Maryland?"

"Yes, that place. That place where we had your birthday."

"Yes, Dad, I'm glad she came home."

"Did she do OK after that? I can't remember."

Annie looked at her frail father. She remembered him standing with her at the formidable double doorway of Belle Grove School for Girls, nestled in the Shenandoah Valley of Virginia. Her mother had tried to take her life again. This time, she had come closer to succeeding. Her father decided home was no longer the right place for Annie. And Annie had been beating the drums about riding lessons. So Belle Grove, where hunt seat riding was secondary only to academics, became the answer. Annie's father gave her a pair of tall riding boots, a velvety hunt cap, several pairs of breeches, and a tweed riding coat before leaving her at Belle Grove.

"Annie?" her father interrupted her thoughts, grasping her arm. "She did OK after that, didn't she?"

"Yes, Dad, she did just fine."

"Good. Now I worry for you. When are you and Tom going to have children? You need children. Women need children."

"We're working on it, Dad."

The old man smiled past Annie, into the distance. "Why are we out here?"

"I just wanted to take you for a walk, Dad, but we can go home now."

"Good, I'm hungry."

The Jeep cruised along at fifty-five miles per hour toward the small town of McCormick. Annie kept an eye on her rearview mirror. She remembered what Tom had said about coming to see Naomi, but she felt sure the dust had settled. The preservation of the Old Lady was yesterday's news.

The campaign for the governorship, on the other hand, was today's big story. Several weeks ago, Porter had seemed to be on the verge of an historic victory. But as election day came closer—only a few days away now—Porter's lead in the polls had been slipping. The issue at hand was, of course, Porter's parentage. The Internet was full of conspiracy theories. What if Porter was not really an American? What if he was an imposter of some kind, sent in to take over the state of South Carolina? The pastor of a megachurch in Columbia had stood in the Sunday pulpit and called Porter "the devil's child." The Republican campaign had watched the controversy unfold, careful not to appear pleased by it, but equally mum when it came to countering the innuendo and firebrand speculation.

"Shit," Annie said out loud. She'd missed a turn.

Annie pulled into a dirt driveway and turned around. A green and white sign said one mile to McCormick. Annie'd gotten Naomi's telephone number from Twig, and Naomi was pleased she was coming.

Naomi lived a few miles on the other side of the city limits of McCormick, such as the city and the limits were. Clearly, McCormick had seen better days. There was the drab beige-on-brown McCormick Motel with an empty swimming pool surrounded by a chain link fence out front. A dilapidated sign announced that the motel offered CLEAN ROOMS, CLEAN SHEETS & AIR CONDITIONING. The R in the word AIR was barely hanging on to the sign.

Annie passed through the middle of town, anchored by a handsome old courthouse and a monument of a Confederate soldier. When she reached the Ritz movie theater, which was closed, she punched in her mileage button. The road to Naomi's house should be five miles down, on the left, marked by a green mailbox with the address 333 North McCormick Highway.

The mailbox stood firmly in the ground. The numbers in 333 stood out clearly. Someone had recently given them a fresh coat of paint.

Annie turned the Jeep onto a small road. It was well maintained, covered with bright, gray gravel that crunched under the Jeep's tires. It meandered through a woody area—mostly tall, skinny pine trees—and then opened into a small, fenced pasture populated by several cows grazing quietly. On the other side of the pasture, Annie could see a small cabin. A trickle of smoke whispered into the air from a brick chimney that rose from one side of the cabin. Chickens wandered around, pecking in the dirt. So this was Naomi's house. The place she talked about coming to as a little girl to see her Grandee.

Annie pulled up in front of the cabin and parked. As she got out of the Jeep, the screen door to the cabin opened.

Naomi was smaller than Annie remembered her. She wore a bright blue dress and a flowery apron. Her hair was gray, pulled back into a small knot at the back of her head. Naomi used a cane. She smiled and raised a thin hand to say hello. Annie took the six steps leading up to Naomi's front porch two at a time and reached for her old friend. The two hugged fiercely.

"I've got someone for you to meet," Naomi said, smiling and resting her hands on Annie's shoulders.

"Who?"

"You'll see."

Behind Naomi, the screen door pushed open again. Annie stared at a handsome man standing in the doorway. Tan skin, green eyes. Henry Porter.

"What are you doing here?" Annie asked, not meaning to sound rude.

"Well, I..."

"He's the baby, Annie," Naomi announced. "The baby born in the barn."

Annie felt light. Not faint, just light, like she could float into the air. Porter reached for her. "Here, you look like you need to sit down."

Porter held Annie's elbow and guided her to a chair on the porch. Annie sat down, breathing slowly. Naomi sat in another chair next to her. Porter stood against the porch railing.

"I don't know what to say," Annie stammered.

"No need to say anything until you're ready," Naomi offered. "I wanted you to know about Henry. I wanted you to see him and meet him. Not like you did at the Old Lady, thinking he was running for governor, but here, knowing he's the baby Twig brought to me."

Annie looked at Naomi and then at Porter.

"Did you know? I mean, when we were trying to save the Old Lady, did you know there was much more to the story than we were telling? Did you know you were born in the barn, on that farm? That we were the ones who brought you into the world? That Twig took you to Naomi? Did you know all that?"

"Yes, I did," Porter said, "but there was no need to discuss it at the time. It was important to save the Old Lady, and thank God we were able to do that."

"But how long have you known? I mean, how long have you known about the circumstances of your birth? Your mother? Your father? And why Porter? Not Portee?"

Naomi spoke up. "That name business was Lily's doings when we went to get the birth certificate. She thought it would be a good idea, to help separate you children from the circumstances and from me. And I told Henry how he was born when he was old enough to understand."

"Have you ever sought out your real mother?" Annie asked Henry. "I mean, you know, I don't mean it like that. Of course Naomi is your mother. But have you ever met Briddy?"

"No, but someday I may."

"What about your father?"

"No again."

Annie stared at Porter.

Naomi patted her hand. "It's a lot to take in, I know, so let me get you something to drink. Something hot? Or something cold?"

"Cold. Real cold."

Naomi disappeared into the small cabin. Porter smiled at Annie. "You know, I can never thank you enough."

"For what?"

"For saving me."

"I didn't save you. I left you out there to die. Then I thought you were dead. Twig saved you."

"No. You all saved me. Briddy, you, Buck, and Twig. You all did something extraordinary.

You managed to take a nightmare and turn it
into a miracle. You gave Briddy a way out. You
gave me a life. You gave my mother the thing
she wanted most. You gave her a child. I can't
think of many things turning out as well as
that, can you?"

"I guess not."

A gentle breeze drifted across the front porch
of the cabin.

"I hope you win," Annie said, "but I have to
wonder how long you can keep the details of
your birth a..."

"A secret?"

"Well, yes, I suppose so. I hate to say it like
that, but that's what it is."

"Seems to me you and your friends have kept it
a secret for a long, long time already."

"Yes, but we aren't public figures. You are."

"And you make a good point. Mama—Naomi—has insisted on handling it from here on out."

"What's she going to do?"

"I'm not altogether sure, but when Mama says she is going to handle something, she handles it. Always has."

Naomi came through the door with a glass of iced tea. She handed it to Annie.

"Here, Mama," Porter said, "you need to sit down now. I'm due back in Charleston by this afternoon, so I've got to be going. I'm sure you and Annie have a lot to talk about."

Henry reached down and kissed Naomi. He gave Annie a hug. "Thanks again," he said, "for everything."

"You're welcome."

Porter walked to the other side of the porch, pulled out his cell phone, and made a call.

Within minutes, a slick, sizable SUV appeared from around the corner.

"Man," Annie said, "that's some kind of service."

"I tell him not to let any of this go to his head," Naomi said. "See that hickory tree over there? Still grows the best switches around. I tell him he's never too old for a lick to the back of the legs if he starts getting too big for his britches."

A trail of dust swirled up behind Porter's car as it made its way down the road away from Naomi's place. Naomi and Annie watched it disappear around the bend. Naomi placed her hand on Annie's arm. It felt cool and small to Annie.

"So tell me, how's my little girl? Have you forgiven me for leaving you like I did?"

"I don't know how to answer that," Annie said quietly. "I was so mad. I was so tired of people leaving me. Sometimes I still get mad about it all."

"I know you were mad, and believe me, I didn't want to do it. If I could have explained it to you, I would have. Oh, dear child, I would have. But I knew I couldn't. I knew, for the sake of the baby, I knew I had to leave. To disappear and not come back. It was the only way at the time. And you had your mama back. It was all I could do. It wasn't perfect. Nothing ever is."

"I know, but Naomi?"

"Yes?"

"Did you ever get to go to college?"

"No, I didn't. I came here with Henry and raised him. There was no time for college. There was no money either."

"Does that bother you?"

"It did at times. When running after a busy little boy and folks wondering why he didn't have a daddy and such as that, yes, I'd get upset. But this community eventually accepted us. Even protected me from the limelight throughout much of this campaign. So does it bother me that I didn't go to college? No, child, because I was meant to raise Henry. And look at him. He has the fine education. He has the means to be anything he wants to be. That's enough for me now. As you get older, you discover you need less. Less of the things you thought you always needed."

"But doesn't it all make you mad? When you look back on things? The way you were treated because you were black? The way your life was defined by a baby that the white world would not have tolerated? That the white world then turned to you to raise? It's just so unfair."

"Unfair? That's a big word. But look at Henry, child. What's unfair about having raised that boy? Having been a part of turning him into a promising young man? I don't think that's unfair. I think that is a gift."

"A gift to you, but what about to South Carolina? He should be the governor, but I am afraid he is going to lose the election because of all the mystery surrounding who he really is. Something's got to give or the election is going to get away from him."

"It's not going anywhere."

"What do you mean?"

"I told Henry after that news conference under the Old Lady that he needed to watch what he was saying or let me say it instead. He got mighty mighty with that reporter. He doesn't need to be doing that."

"Then what should he do?"

"He should let me do it. Let me say what I need to say when I need to say it. And that will be soon, I think. You'll see. Everybody will see. But tell me about you."

"Well, there's not a whole lot to say. Mama died a few years ago. Daddy's still alive, but he has Alzheimer's. I saw him the other day and he thinks I'm still married. He wants to know when I'm going to have children. I'm living out at Lake Murray, doing my art."

"Living by yourself?"

"I have a cat."

"You know what I mean."

"Yes, I'm single. I live alone."

"I hate that."

"Why? You live alone."

"I know I do, but you and I are different. I got used to taking care of myself a long, long time ago. I believe the only person I'd ever let share my space would be if Luke came back to life. But even he'd have to mind his Ps and Qs. I'm an old lady used to living by myself. I've got my ways and I don't like anybody monkeying with them. Now you, on the other hand, don't need to get too used to that."

"Well, I'm going to see Buck soon. He lives in North Carolina, on a mountain. He's a vet *and* he's single."

"And that's the best news I've heard all day."

Naomi squeezed Annie's hand. A bluebird landed on a fence post nearby.

"Now, look at that," the old woman said, pointing an arthritic finger at the winged creature. "Grandee used to say that's the bluest blue in the world. Bluer than the sky. Bluer than the ocean. And do you know, Annie, why God made that color blue? And why he painted it on a shy little bird?"

"No, I don't."

"To remind you that beauty is always around you. It's in the air, it's getting ready to land nearby. But you've got to keep your eyes open, baby. You've got to keep your eyes open for it. Fact is, though, I suspect you've already seen it."

"Seen what?"

Naomi drew back in her chair and smiled. "Why, the beauty."

"You mean the bluebird?"

"No, I mean Buck."

CHAPTER TWENTY

Annie'd just gotten back from the grocery store when her cell phone rang. She dropped her bags on the floor and fished it out of her back pocket. Maybe it was Buck, Annie thought, feeling like a lovestruck teenager.

"Hello?"

"Oh, my God! Are you watching the news?"

It was Dorsey on the other end of the line.

"What news?"

"The news on TV. Turn it on, quick."

"But..."

"Just turn on the television. Channel ten. Something's going on with the Porter campaign. Something big. I'll call you when it's over. Bye."

Click.

Annie went to the den and turned on the television. It was already on the right channel. A woman was standing in a grassy area. Behind her was a cabin. A cabin, Annie thought, that looked a lot like Naomi's.

Forgetting the groceries, Annie sat down on the sofa. She thought immediately of Naomi's recent contention that she would soon take a stand of some kind in her son's campaign. *Let me say what I need to say when I need to say it.*

Annie watched the woman on the television. She was the reporter for WIS-TV News. Diane

Wise. She adjusted her jacket, took a last look at her notes, and began talking into the camera.

"We're here in McCormick, South Carolina, about forty-five miles due west of Columbia. A press conference has been called by the Porter campaign to begin shortly, in front of this small cabin. Though we have been assured that the press conference will begin at noon sharp, we have not seen signs of anyone inside the cabin. Nor have we seen any sign of Henry Porter, who is running an historic campaign to become the first black governor of South Carolina. According to my watch, the press conference should begin in about ten minutes."

"Diane?" a voice said off-camera. It was the news anchor back at the Columbia station.

"Yes, Ben?"

"Is there any information concerning what this press conference is about?"

"No, Ben, there isn't. Porter's press secretary, John Hatch, will only say that no questions will be taken after the press conference is over, but he wouldn't say who is actually holding the press conference or what it's about. All very mysterious."

"Is there any *speculation* about the subject of the press conference?"

"Well, Ben, as you know, the question of who Porter's mother and father are has become a real problem for the campaign. People want to know, and perhaps today, in front of this small cabin out in the country, we are going to find out."

"Perhaps so," Ben said. "I'll let you go so you can get set up."

"Thank you, Ben. We won't let our viewers miss a thing."

The camera switched to a shoulders-and-head shot of Ben at the anchor desk. "If you're just tuning in, a press conference has been called by the Porter campaign..."

Annie looked at her watch. She ran to the kitchen and put the butter, milk, and cheese in the refrigerator. Everything else could wait. She returned to the den.

The television showed a still shot of the cabin. Yes, it was definitely Naomi's place. Annie could see the straight-back pine chair that she had sat in on the front porch during her recent visit there.

Dumbfounded and her heart racing, Annie watched as the cabin's screen door opened slowly. Naomi, holding her cane in one hand, stepped into the cameras' lights. She stood on the front porch. She wore a housedress, a sweater, and a pair of tennis shoes. Her gray hair was pulled into the same tight knot that it had been arranged in when Annie had seen her.

"Oh, my God," Annie murmured.

Naomi looked around at the reporters and walked up to a grouping of microphones that stood together in a tall arrangement on the top step of the porch. When Naomi moved, cameras began clicking. Naomi stepped back, surprised but not deterred.

"Which one of these things do I talk into?" she asked, moving forward again and pointing to the microphones.

"Just talk," said someone in the crowd of media. "They'll pick up your voice."

"I suppose they will," Naomi groused.

"Well, then," Naomi began, "I am glad you all could come today, but I am not glad you have parked your vehicles all over my yard. I work hard to grow my grass, and if it's all torn up, I'm going to be mighty upset."

There was a ripple of nervous laughter from the press corps.

"Of course, I don't believe any of you came here today to hear me talk about my grass, now did you?"

Silence.

"Well, did you? Because if you did, that's what we'll talk about."

Several reporters looked at one another, and then one said, "Well, no, ma'am, we didn't come to hear you talk about your grass. But we don't know what you're going to talk about. Will you tell us?"

Naomi narrowed her eyes at the reporter who'd spoken.

"What's your name, son?"

"Will Murphy, with the Associated Press."

"Well, Mr. Will Murphy With The Associated Press, that's some name you have."

More nervous laughter.

"Will works fine," Murphy said. "And what is your name?"

"Mrs. Naomi Portee."

"Well, Mrs. Portee, can you tell us why we are here today?"

"I suppose I can."

Naomi shifted, setting her feet just a little farther apart. She placed her cane in front of her, leaning on it with both hands, one on top of the other. She looked diminutive behind the tangled bouquet of microphones, but nevertheless, determined.

"I am here today to tell you something about Henry Porter."

A firestorm of cameras clicked.

"After I have told you all I am going to tell you, I am going to go right back where I came from.

I am going through the door of my cabin, and I
am going to eat a piece of cold cornbread and a
bowl of warm vegetable soup. Then I am going
to take a nap, and I am not going to come back
out here until you have all left. I am not going
to answer any of your questions because one
thing I know about you all, other than you
park where you aren't supposed to, is that
your questions never end. So I will end them
for you by going back inside my house when I
have said what I have to say. Now, let me catch
my breath."

Naomi stood quietly, breathing in the crisp
air of the early November day, gathering her
thoughts.

The reporters waited just as quietly, mesmerized by the resolute woman and by a press conference unlike any they had ever encountered.

"I am an old lady. I don't have any money to
speak of, but I don't know that I need it either. I
do have this cabin and this small patch of land
you're standing on. My grandmama gave it to
me, and I have treasured it all my life. Inside my

cabin, you won't find much. A few sticks of furniture. A stove. A sink. A bed with a mattress that sinks to the middle. And a bathroom. I own a TV. I don't care for most of what comes across it— it's trash and it's terrible—but I do like to watch the news. That is how I know you are all wondering who Henry Porter's mama and daddy are. I also know Mr. Porter says it's none of your business, but I'm not so sure about that. Maybe it is. Maybe each and every one of you, and each and every one of the folks who casts their votes for governor next week, should know a little something about how Henry Porter came to be. And I'm going to tell you.

"But before I go any further, I want to say this: I never want to see as many people gathered around my little cabin as I do right now, and the first one of you that puts a foot on my porch steps is going to wish he or she hadn't done so. This cane can do a whole lot more than hold me up, if you know what I mean."

The press corps moved ever so slightly backward. Annie smiled.

"But this gathering isn't about me. It's about Mr. Porter. Who he is and where he came from. Of course, I like to call him Henry because from the time he was born, I fed him, bathed him, praised him, taught him, and, when he was old enough to start learning right from wrong, I took a hickory stick to the back of his legs when it was necessary. So most folks, I believe, would say Henry is my son.

"But Henry did not grow in my belly and slide out between my legs. He came, instead, by way of two very young people who, at the time, had no business falling in love and having a baby. They were children themselves. They weren't married. But more difficult than all that, one of them was white and the other was black. So when Henry came into the world, he had no place to go, and he was brought to me. Henry came wrapped in a sweatshirt. The bearer of this baby—a person who was brave and determined to see that this child had a home—said something that has stuck in my gut and never gone away. He placed the bundle in my arms and he said, 'Here, Naomi, you gotta take it.

You just gotta take it.' And that's what I did. I took that baby.

"So who are Henry Porter's mama and daddy? They are our shared history. They are what it means to have grown up in a time in our country when white people and black people didn't mix and woe be to them that did. But those parents are also what it means to fall in love despite all that, to yearn for the warmth of another's arms despite the color of those arms. So they are what it means to go against the grain, to reach out despite every danger, every admonition, every prejudiced thought, word, and deed. And to my way of thinking, that is a good thing. But at the time, it was the wrong thing.

"So, as I said, Henry was born—the color of coffee ice cream—and he was brought to me. I did not expect him, but I took him. I went down to the vital records office in Columbia with a friend and my baby boy and I told them he was born at home and that his last name was Porter. I don't really know why I did that, but I was scared. Never felt so scared in my life. But then with that baby, I had such strength. I had the whole world bundled up in my arms. I felt a certain weight too. The weight of a world that has worked hard to keep skin colors separate, the weight of a young man who likely did not know he had become a father, the weight of a young mother who knew not what to do, and the weight of that fine baby boy.

"So all you gathered here can spread what I'm fixing to tell you as far and wide as you want with your cameras and computers and recorders and microphones and whatnot. Henry was a gift from God. He came with a lesson the good Lord so wants to get through to us. We need to accept that we are all the same. It doesn't matter what color skin we walk around in. Or what side of town we come from. Or who our mama is or who our daddy is. It only matters what we do. What we do to help each other. What we do to make this world better. What we do to love.

"So that's who Henry is. He's black and he's white. He came from a time that wasn't ready for him. He came from a place that had no home for him. And he is you and he is me, and he is everything that has gone on in this world so far, and he is the future of how it could be if we all put our minds to being one, instead of this fancy person and that not-fancy person, this color and that color, this religion and that religion, this difference and that difference. And that is all I've got to say. Now, I'm going inside to have my soup."

Naomi turned from the cameras. She planted her cane in front of her, took a step, and then another, toward the screen door. When she reached for the handle, Will Murphy jumped forward onto the porch, opening the door for Naomi.

"Thank you," Naomi said to him. "I said I'd go after anybody that came up here, but that was mighty nice of you, Mr. Will Murphy With The Associated Press."

Naomi disappeared into the small cabin.

Annie wiped several tears from her face. The
phone rang. It would be Dorsey, but Annie did
not pick it up. She would call him back later.

The picture on the television screen changed
from the empty front porch of Naomi's cabin to
a shot of the WIS-TV reporter, who had moved
away from the crowd of media and was standing in front of a fence that separated Naomi's
yard from a pasture.

Annie did not hear what the reporter was
saying.

Instead, she watched a bluebird land ever so
briefly on the wooden railing and then take
flight.